# The Betrayed

## A Newport Murder Mystery

Maria Milot

For my husband, who makes all things possible.

# ONE

Maddie desperately clawed at the large hands digging into her neck, crushing her throat. Her eyes opened wide with panic as she fought to inhale. She jolted upright with a loud gasp. Maddie twisted her head and searched but there was no sign of the faceless man choking the life out of her; just the familiar comfort of the couch she had fallen asleep on. She took in a few more desperate gasps of relief, stood up and padded barefoot across the tight, scratchy bumps of a sisal rug.

She rubbed her throat as she looked out the large French doors in her living room, trying to shake off the shockingly real feelings that lingered from her late afternoon dream. Her mind churned with worry as her eyes scanned the panorama of the ocean just beyond a worn slate patio and the early blooms of the June garden. *Oh, Mr. Whitmore I really need you to tell me everything will be okay. I miss you,* she thought.

Maddie was safe inside her stone cottage tucked onto the former Firestone family estate known as Ocean Lawn. The main house, which had been subdivided into condominiums, was only about sixty yards away. *Surely, someone would be home to help me in an emergency,* she thought.

Looking out at an orange swath painted across the shimmering water she felt a wave of peace come over her. Her breath became soft and steady. The corner of her thumb stopped burrowing under her fingernails as her anxiety faded. *It's magic hour, Mr. Whitmore, thanks.*

Twilight, it was a time of possibilities, when the bright light of the day softened to reveal new colors in the sky. She always felt hopeful at this time of day. Something about the half-light illuminated all the

1

possibilities of the night ahead; possibly slipping into well-worn sweats for a quiet evening with a book and a large glass of chardonnay. The memory of her dream slipped from her mind as she pondered the potential of the night ahead. Perhaps a dinner out with Winston. Her world had changed over the past year. It had been a long time since she had dated a man but now that had changed too. She smiled as she watched the orange sky turn to a brilliant fuchsia streaked with purple.

Her phone buzzed on the marble kitchen counter indicating a new text message. She turned away from the twinkling lights appearing on the opposite shore against the now mostly indigo sky. An invitation out, yes, but it was her friend Kelly hoping to catch up over drinks.

Maddie shook off her shorts and tee shirt and pulled on a pale blue dress. She slid the thin spaghetti straps up over her tanned shoulders. Partly to spite Joe but mostly to try to remember her own preferences, she had stocked her wardrobe full of blue. Joe hated blue but it had always been her favorite color and all shades of it complimented her smooth Mediterranean skin.

Still barefoot she walked through her kitchen. She did not allow shoes to be worn in her home. Just the thought of walking on the germs brought in by shoes made her toes curl. She stepped onto the cool slate of her mudroom floor, slipped into a pair of sandals and grabbed her keys. She embraced the warm night as she took a deep breath of the slightly salty, heavy, humid air. *This will be good,* she told herself as she prepared for summer in Newport with all its possibilities.

# TWO

It was well after sunset. His lips softly pulled back from the kiss. He let his hand drop down to caress the bare chest of the other man.

"How about a drink?" he asked, using the frame of the boat's wide double berth to push himself up off his lover.

"Whatever you're having," responded the man still stretched out on the bed.

He walked over to the galley and poured them each a Scotch.

"So, when are you ever going to take me on a date?" The man asked as he sat up on the bed.

He suddenly turned from the galley counter. "Hey! You know that can't happen." Bottle in hand he gestured at the man still lounging as he continued to admonish. "I have made it very clear to you no one can ever find out about this, about us. Not only is it inappropriate, it could ruin everything I have."

"Alright." The man on the bed surrendered his hands up in the air. "It's just, you know, times have changed. This isn't the seventies."

"Yes, times have changed," he replied walking toward the bed with the drinks. "Just not for me. Now, if you like what we have you will drink this, shut your mouth, and follow my orders."

The man on the bed looked up into his eyes. "Yes sir, you're the boss."

He knew what the man on the bed wanted but it was getting late. He had early morning plans and needed to get some rest. He bent down and let his tongue glide across the waiting lips of his lover. "Finish your drink; it's time for you to go. I'll set something up for us mid-week."

The man on the bed took a big swig of his whiskey, got up and dressed. He plucked a cell phone from the pile of clothing he was putting on and waved it. "See I have the phone you gave me. I never go anywhere without it, just in case you need me."

"And you never, ever use that phone except for us?" he asked.

"Yes, sir. I understand the rules. I use my own cell phone for all other business and this one is yours, just yours," the man answered as he finished getting dressed.

"Good," he said. "Now get out. I'll contact you on that line around Wednesday."

A smirk beamed across the man's face as he stepped off the boat onto the dock. A part of him desperately wanted more from the man he just left. But a part of him tingled knowing that he was leading a secret life with this very public man.

# THREE

The drive downtown to Thames Street, Newport's main shopping and dining area, took just a few minutes in her metallic-grey Audi A8. *No valet for you, Silver Bullet, let's see if I can find you a spot,* Maddie thought as she drove into the parking lot at the Moorings Restaurant.

Until recently she had scrapped and saved every dime just to afford a basic used car. Her luxury vehicle still had its new car smell, leaving her reluctant to let someone else drive it away. She locked her car and checked around for Kelly's Jeep. However, summer in Newport meant more than one Jeep Wrangler in the parking lot.

The restaurant was situated, partially on wooden pilings, over Newport's inner harbor on Sayers Wharf. Maddie climbed the stone steps and was greeted inside the door by a young, slender woman with long blonde hair and lots of suntan showing around her pink and white Lily Pulitzer dress. Summer in Newport; so many beautiful people ready to see and be seen.

"Good Evening. Table for one?" the girl asked.

"Oh no. I'm meeting a friend," Maddie answered, pointing to the hall on the right which led to the lounge.

Walking into the bar was like stepping onto a classic, old ship. The space was dominated by a varnished wood bar. Its brass tap fixtures glowed under dim nautical lighting. An eclectic mix of casually well-dressed people dotted the seating.

As Maddie walked further into the room, heads turned her way. Men checking her over was not a new experience. Once, she had felt flattered by compliments but now she wanted to melt into the polished paneling.

At five foot three, she was slim and petite and easily slid past the bar stools to get a full look at the room. *Oh, thank God, there she is,* she thought as she spotted a flash of Kelly's strawberry-blonde hair at the opposite end of the oblong bar.

Kelly was sipping a white wine and waved. Maddie raised her hand in response and headed around the corner and down the long side of the bar, not oblivious to the eyes following her. Her appearance had always drawn attention, but it was an air of compassion and caring emanating from her that caused people to want to stay around. Her circle of friends counted on her to be the listener and mediator between people. That was back when she had more than one friend.

Kelly hopped off her bar stool. Wearing flat shoes, she was five foot eight. She hunched over to give her friend a big hug then whipped her head around and signaled the bartender for two more chardonnays.

"Two, who else is joining us?" Maddie asked.

"No one. I just don't want downtime between my drinks." Kelly smiled mischievously. Her chin length hair, cut at an angle, framed her face with its small features, fair skin and light freckles sprinkled across her nose; which was now scrunched up as she laughed and sipped again from her half-filled wine glass.

Maddie had known Kelly Hurley since nursing school. Kelly was the first person Maddie had called, even before her own sister, when her mother had passed away two years ago from a heart attack. Having watched her father suffer and succumb to cancer ten years prior to her mother's death was the reason Maddie had become a nurse.

Kelly's father had also passed away when she was in seventh grade, one of the many things Kelly and Maddie had in common.

"Wow, look at you, Madison Marcelle, carrying a fancy Hermes bag. I guess life is pretty different since you inherited all that money."

Maddie shifted on the bar stool, looked down, and tucked her hair behind her ear. Kelly could tell she had made her friend feel uncomfortable.

"I'm just giving you a hard time, Maddie. Seriously, I am so happy for you. I mean you've always worked hard. You're kind, generous with your time and now you can be generous with your money too! Drinks on you, right?"

A genuine smile spread across Maddie's face. "Absolutely!"

"So, really, Maddie, how have you been doing?" asked Kelly.

Maddie shrugged. "You mean since Mr. Whitmore died eight months ago and my life completely changed? Well, for starters, I really miss him."

"Of course you do. You were with him every day for nearly three years. He obviously loved you like family; which is why he left you all his money. Did you ever have any idea he had so much?"

Maddie's eyes opened wide. "Never! When I interviewed to be his private nurse it was in that little house in Jamestown. He had me running errands in his Oldsmobile from twenty years ago. I just assumed he was living lean with a good insurance policy. I almost didn't take the job, but then he told me a silly joke about cheese."

"And there it is, Maddie; I know you have a penchant for stupid jokes." Kelly drained her first wine and dipped right into the next glass.

"Exactly! We just clicked. He was so funny. He had so much wisdom. I became his family and truly he became mine."

Kelly signaled the bartender for two more chardonnays. "Umm, what about your sister?"

"Oh please. What about your sister Kelly? Face it, our sisters live nowhere near us, they are never around when we need them, and you will remember that mine didn't even show up for our mother's funeral. She just sent some flowers! So, let's leave it that for all practical purposes I am an only child. Besides, Mr. Whitmore was there for me when everything went down with Joe."

"I'm sorry Maddie that was such an awful situation. You were so poised during that mess, just taking your stuff and getting out. I would have trashed the place and slashed his tires. But for everything we have in common, I guess that's one area we differ. I'm more suspicious and vindictive."

Maddie nodded up and down. "I know, that's why I'm never on your bad side. Well thankfully, Mr. Whitmore took me in and let me live with him. As much as I took care of him, he took care of me too. He was a like father to me and we had fun together." A smile came over Maddie's face as she remembered her friend and benefactor.

"Hey, speaking of fun, how is the Disney Prince?" Kelly asked.

Maddie threw her head back and laughed. "He does look like a Disney Prince. I think his teeth twinkled when I met him. I guess meeting Winston is another thing I can thank Mr. Whitmore for."

"Did you meet him at Mr. Whitmore's?"

"No, I met him at Anderson and Anderson, the law firm, while I was waiting for my appointment to find out about Mr. Whitmore's will. I think my mouth dropped open and drool came out when he said 'hello' to me. He was so-painfully handsome. I'm not sure what I babbled about. I don't even think I gave him my phone number. The next thing I knew the senior partners were signaling him. He told me he wanted to continue our conversation and asked if I was available for drinks later. I thought I just watched his mouth move, but apparently, I agreed to something before he vanished into his meeting."

"So, what happened, how did Winston find you?"

"I'm still not sure how he got in touch with me because right after he walked away I was called in to see Mr. Whitmore's lawyer, Jeffrey Shorey."

Kelly swirled the wine around in her glass. "So you had no idea what was in store?"

"No. Mr. Shorey told me Mr. Whitmore had updated his will and I was his sole heir. I thought it meant I would get the old car and the little house in Jamestown. Honestly, I was thinking I could probably sell the house make some good money, given the property values in Jamestown, then start looking for another job. Instead, he told me not

9

only was I getting the house and the car but I was also getting tens of millions of dollars." Maddie took a long sip from her glass.

Kelly's eyes opened wide. "So were you excited or shocked?"

"I remember sitting there, staring at this ficus tree behind his desk. All I could focus on were these three yellow leaves dangling from a bottom branch, trying to hang on to the life they used to have flowing through them. Then a glass of water appeared in front of me." Maddie closed her eyes and once again was sitting in the office of Jeff Shorey.

*"Here, you need this." Jeff handed her a glass. She took the water and started to cry.*

"It just hit me, Kelly, all of it, Mr. Whitmore's death, the money. I had all this information blowing around inside my head, like a brain blizzard. I couldn't see through it to figure any of it out."

*Jeff Shorey had placed a gentle hand on Maddie's shoulder, "You don't need to worry, Miss Marcelle. I can handle everything, I was Mr. Whitmore's attorney for a very long time, and I would be honored to continue as yours."*

Maddie took another sip before she continued. "Then he started talking about asset distribution, if I wanted to sell the house, if I wanted to buy a new house, if I wanted advice on investments, if I wanted to set up an estate plan. I mean there was so much to think about. My head was spinning, almost literally because he stopped talking, smiled and told me to relax; I didn't have to decide anything right there. He suggested we get together in a couple days to map out a plan, and not to worry. Then he handed me an envelope."

10

*Maddie gave Jeff Shorey a quizzical look, "What is this?"*

*"Mr. Whitmore wanted to be sure you had some 'walking around money' after he was gone. The money in this envelope should more than cover groceries, gas, whatever you need until everything is sorted out."*

"Of course, I started to cry again. Mr. Shorey was so calm and patient. He reminded me of Mr. Whitmore; which reminded me that Mr. Whitmore was really gone."

"You never told me all that, Maddie."

"I know. I just wasn't ready to talk about it yet."

"And you still haven't told me about that first date with Winston."

"What can I say? He was a rock for me that day. When I left the lawyer's office, I was a mess. Somehow he got my phone number. He could tell I was upset and told me he could help. He directed me to a bar about a block away from Anderson and Anderson. He was everything I needed. A good listener and a good advisor. He's apparently qualified because he's not just rich, he's filthy rich. His family, the Coopers, are Anderson and Anderson's biggest client."

Kelly put down her glass and slapped her hands on the bar. "Wait, Winston's last name is Cooper? As in, THE Coopers? You do realize they are famous around here, right? I read about them all the time in the Rhode Island magazines. There's always a picture of James

Cooper, older guy but really good looking. I think they're old money, like the Vanderbilts and Astors."

"Yeah, James is Winston's dad. Turns out their money goes back to the late 1800s. 'The Gilded Age' he called it. Anderson and Anderson has been doling out the trust fund from generation to generation of his family."

Kelly frowned. "I'm surprised the money hasn't been used up."

"Well, it seems Winston's dad was some kind of Wall Street wizard. He brought the family's dwindling millions back up to billions. He's retired but he still manages the family money."

Kelly leaned closer to Maddie. "From what I've heard James definitely has a passion for control and a knack for making money; where Winston seems to have a passion for leisure and a knack for spending money."

Maddie shrugged her shoulders. "All I know is that we spent hours in that bar, sharing stories. When he finally walked me to my car I felt good but I knew I would feel better if I could see him again." Maddie sat up a little straighter and steeled herself before she continued. "Yes, and because of what happened with Joe I'm trying very hard to keep things casual and moving slowly." She knew this was the right thing to tell Kelly. Kelly, who was always so strong and in control. Kelly would never allow herself to emotionally depend on anyone, man or woman. Which is why it was so hard to talk to her sometimes. Months of sleepless nights led her to the next words she uttered to Kelly. "I don't want to jump into an exclusive relationship that I get lost in, and then it destroys me, again." *There I said it aloud,* she thought letting out an audible sigh of relief.

Kelly's shoulders shifted in a quick shrug as she said, "Well it's good that you're keeping your options open." Unaware of the milestone Maddie had just reached by admitting she was ready to explore dating. "I can't believe I didn't put together Winston is a Cooper; although his dad is usually the one to monopolize the media. Just be careful. Winston's family isn't just rich; they're powerful. As much as you wouldn't want to be on my bad side, I wouldn't want to be on their bad side."

Maddie took another long drink of wine. "Enough about me. What's going on with you and Jack? Have you set a wedding date yet?"

"Turns out setting a date is part of a chain reaction. Right now Jack is up for a promotion, so we're waiting to see how that will play out with his hours and vacation time."

"What kind of promotion? I mean as long as I can remember Jack's been a cop."

"Yeah, he loves being on the streets. But now that we're settling down, and someday hope to have children, he's thinking a few steps ahead. You know he's always had great instincts, he's smart, and a position has opened up for a detective on the squad."

"Wow! Congratulations!" exclaimed Maddie. "How do you feel about this?"

"I'm thrilled! Even though we live in Newport, not New York City, I still worry when he goes out on his shift. I mean, you just never know what might happen out there. At least this way the plan is for him to investigate crimes after they've happened not be a part of them in progress. Again, there are no safety guarantees anywhere in his line of work, but it does give me some peace of mind. Besides the position change comes with a pay raise," Kelly added with a smile. "The other piece of the wedding puzzle involves trying to get a date at the church. We're really hoping to get married at St. Mary's, given that it's the oldest Catholic Church in Rhode Island. But, since President Kennedy married Jackie there, it's always in demand and the church books way more than a year in advance. In fact, there's a link on their website dedicated to all the restrictions and rules that need to be followed in order to have a ceremony there."

"Restrictive rules for the Catholic church, you don't say?" Maddie commented facetiously.

"Hey, I am a practicing Catholic and my Irish ancestors literally laid the bricks and stones to build that church," Kelly scowled.

Maddie sincerely apologized. "I'm sorry. You know I'm not very religious but I should be respectful."

Kelly nodded an acceptance then suggested, "Maybe we should have our wedding at your new house? It's pretty posh living up there among the mansions, with a view that I'll never be able to afford."

"Kelly, if you and Jack need help with money-"

"Oh no!" Kelly interjected. "I was just kidding. You are such a good friend. Jack and I know we can always count on you, but we really are okay. Besides what if the situation was reversed, hmm?"

"You're right," Maddie conceded. "We were both raised to be self-sufficient and proud of it. I think that's one of the reasons I'm having such a hard time figuring out what to do next." She wanted to tell Kelly the other reasons she was having a hard time. Like how the quiet of living alone made her jump at every noise. How she had taken to napping in the afternoon because she couldn't sleep at night, convinced someone was lurking in the dark. Or the dreams that woke her up either gasping for air or smothered under a pall of loss and death, the only release coming from a good, hard cry. She felt she was on a balance beam of emotion. Putting one foot in front of the other required constant concentration. Her feelings teetered from guilt for giving up her career to happiness for having it all. And way down there was fear. Fear she would lose everyone close to her and have no one to share it all with. But she had told her friend enough. Kelly was strong, and any more talk of paranoid, overthought, or squishy feelings from Maddie would have Kelly slapping her on the arm and telling her to 'move on!'

"Maddie, things happen for a reason. This is your time to do all the stuff we always talk about doing. And until now, you haven't looked at a man since Joe. Go out with Winston. Be open to meeting new men.

Have fun. Spend money. When you're ready, you will find something you can refocus your energy into and you'll have some perspective." Maddie bobbed her head up and down in agreement. Kelly signaled for the check. "Come on let's go over to the Clarke Cooke House and see what's going on over there."

They made the short walk, cutting through the brick alley that linked Sayers Wharf to the adjacent Bannisters Wharf, and joined the sophisticated but rowdy crowd gathered inside the Cooke House.

# FOUR

Bob Lackey had always been a good-looking kid and he used it to his advantage. He had his father's Irish blue eyes and his mother's dark brown, almost black, thick Sicilian hair and dark olive skin. Even in elementary school girls wanted to be around him. He quickly figured out how to use his charm to get girls to give up everything from the pudding cup in their lunchbox to their babysitting cash. As a small boy, he lived in Cranston until his parents divorced when he was ten. After that, he saw little of his dad. His mom, Marie, moved them up to Federal Hill to live with her mother.

Just like Rome, the city of Providence is built on seven hills; Federal Hill being one. Also like Rome, Federal Hill, or *The Hill* as it is referred to by locals, is populated by Italians. Between 1900 and 1930 a wave of immigrants invaded The Hill, turning the area into Providence's own "Little Italy." Atwells Avenue, the wide main *corso,* street, of The Hill was lined with mostly three-story wood and brick buildings. The grid of adjoining structures was divided into narrow streets and small alleyways. Just like in The Old Country, business was conducted on the street level and the upper few floors of the buildings were used as residences.

As Bob walked along Atwells Avenue he glanced into the many restaurants, boutiques, and small Italian food markets; waving to a couple of older *paisans* standing outside the market where his mother used to work. Although the neighborhood had changed little since he was a kid, his relationship with the people in charge here certainly had.

When he got to the liquor store he paused and looked up at the windows above a dark green awning; surveying the apartment where he had spent most of his life. His grandmother had long since passed and his mother was now in a condo down in Florida. But twenty-two years ago this is where he began his association with the organization. An organization that now put a nauseating knot in his stomach.

# FIVE

Boom- boom- boom- boom, Maddie's head was pounding like the music from the night before down in the appropriately named Boom Boom Room on the bottom level of the Clarke Cooke House. Her hands went to her forehead as she realized that her tongue was bound to the roof of her mouth. She forced it to peel away with a twacking sound. She probed her tongue around to be sure she hadn't actually slept with a roll of gauze in her mouth. Maddie dragged herself to the bathroom and slurped directly from the faucet, then swallowed down three aspirin tablets. *Now I remember why Kelly and I don't do this more often. Next time one wine, one water, one wine, one water. And God bless Jack for showing up so Kelly could drive me home. That girl must have a hollow leg!*

She gingerly walked to the kitchen, holding her head again to be sure her brain didn't thump out. She looked over her K-cup packs next to the coffee maker, hoping there was a brew named Hangover Strong. Slowly, she eased onto a tall leather chair, rested her elbows on the kitchen island, sipped her coffee, stared at the ocean, and waited for part one of her hangover cure to kick in.

# SIX

On the surface, it seemed the only means of financial support for his family had come from his mother's part-time job at the market. Yet she never seemed worried about money. Growing up, Bob always had name brand clothes and the latest high-end sneakers. Marie pampered herself with regular manicures, pedicures, and spa treatments. Every weekend she would go out wearing lavish outfits. Bob, rightfully, attributed their good fortune to his mother's friend, Frank Armondetta. Often, he would come home from school to find Mr. Armondetta sitting at his mother's kitchen table. Frank had a soft spot for Bob. He would ruffle Bob's hair and tell him he could make a little money for himself delivering and picking up envelopes around the neighborhood and returning them to Marie.

Bob was no stranger to violence. He worked to keep his always hot temper tamped down to a simmer. Mr. Armondetta made sure Bob never took any real heat for the street scuffles he got in as a teen. He kept him from doing any time when he was twenty-one, despite choking and beating a man in a bar fight. Bob seemed to have garnered value around the neighborhood partly because that was the nature of the Federal Hill community. It was a place where everyone was connected by family, by business, or both. In fact, it was the connection between his mother and Mr. Armondetta that allowed Bob the illusion of respect. Frank Armondetta ran this town.

Mr. Armondetta was the *capo,* head, of his family's powerful organization. Although Bob was never a true part of the business, Marie saw to that. Not for lack of trying, Bob was never a Made Man. He never ran with a crew. He was considered an associate, a friend of the

20

family, and as such he was afforded certain privileges. Like being able to run his mouth off in bars about sleeping with a buddy's girlfriend and not getting popped, or borrowing money for the almost bi-monthly benders down at the Connecticut casinos. Mr. Armondetta even bought Bob a condominium on Newport Harbor, and a tricked out thirty-foot power boat. A purchase Bob was convinced would get him even more 'ass from da ladies.'

But life had changed drastically in the last five years. It started when Frank was given a terminal sentence from lung cancer. Frank gave Marie a hefty retirement sum and sent her to Florida. Then he prepared to pass the family business to his nephew, Cosimo DeCastelleri; also known as Mr. D. Mr. Armondetta assured Bob he would still be considered a friend of the family.

Bob continued his trek up the avenue. His hands were hot and damp but not from the summer heat. He wiped the moisture building on his palms along the sides of his charcoal grey trousers. Yes, Bob was confident his charisma would work on the ladies but he was not at all sure his charm would work with Mr. D.

Sounds of accordion music wafted through the hot, gritty city air. When he reached the middle of Atwells Avenue, Bob turned to his left and walked into an Old World cobblestone piazza. In the center of the piazza was a large stone fountain. Water was bubbling, flowing, and spilling over the sides of its three round tiers. The sound of the splashing water offered a cool respite from the stifling heat of the day. Tourists and locals strolled around, some sitting on the edge of the fountain eating gelato, many lounging under umbrella-shaded tables at outdoor cafes and restaurants that lined the perimeter of the piazza. Enormous embellished stone urns surrounded the piazza, vibrant with magenta flowers. DePasquale Square was the heart of Federal Hill.

Bob passed the traditional Italian marketplace which anchored a corner of the square and continued toward the rear of the plaza. He snaked his way through the lively action of De Pasquale Square toward a small black door between two popular eateries. As he pressed a button on the door he looked around at the visitors in the square, most of whom were unaware that just above their heads, behind a center window overlooking the picturesque pinecone fountain, was a dark and dangerous domain.

The door buzzed open and Bob stepped inside. The air felt cool but still smelled of herbs and grease from the surrounding restaurants. The light radiating from a large glass chandelier hanging over the middle of the staircase in front of him was much dimmer than the bright sunshine outside. He let his eyes adjust for a second and then ascended the steep steps. As he passed under the chandelier two men rose up from spindle-backed wooden armchairs atop the stair landing. From a distance they looked much like him, well-groomed Italian gentlemen with dark, slicked-back hair and dark fitted suits. But as Bob drew closer he could see their faces showed evidence of broken noses and scars from fights that no gentleman would be in. The men moved aside the lapels of their jackets to reveal their shoulder holsters. Bob gave his name and appointment time to the two men guarding a door set at the back of the hallway. One of the men picked up a clipboard from a small table between the chairs. Bob noted the chairs were not designed for comfort, just convenience for the men stationed outside of Mr. D's office.

"What's ya numbuh?" asked the Clipboard Guard in a heavy Rhode Island accent, void of the letter 'r' at the end of a word.

"Oh, yeah, ah, two, three, fowah," Bob answered the guard, in his own Rhode Island accent. The number he gave identified him and allowed him access to the office, not a trip to the hospital.

"Mr. DeCastelleri is expecting you. He should be finished in a couple minutes," was the gruff confirmation from the guard with the clipboard.

22

While they waited in silence, Bob looked back down the stairs. He hoped he would walk back down those steps and not be thrown down them once Mr. D found out he was not here to pay but to ask for more time to get the money.

Bob was used to slipping in shit and landing in gold. Right now standing in the hall outside of this office, waiting for what was on the other side, he knew he was pretty deep in the shit.

The office door swung open. The blonde man exiting the office still had his hand on the knob with his head turned over his shoulder calling into the office. "Thanks, Cosimo, I'll let you know when it's done." The blonde man turned and walked out the door brushing past Bob as if he were just another sentry, then swaggered down the stairs.

One of the sharp dressed men standing between Bob and the door announced, "Mr. Lackey is here to see you now Mr. D."

"Send him in," replied Cosimo DeCastelleri.

Bob stepped through the door. *Showtime.*

# SEVEN

Two cups of coffee, three glasses of water, and one hot shower later Maddie was ready for the final step of her hangover cure--fresh air. She strolled off the grounds of her home onto Narragansett Avenue and glanced around. *Not too many tourist cars parked here today,* she thought. Before going down the Forty Steps access point to Newport's famed Cliff Walk she wondered how much of a hike she could handle. To her left it was a fairly short, and easy, shot to the start of Cliff Walk; overlooking Easton's Beach, also known as First Beach. Perched high above First Beach was the elegant Chanler hotel and restaurant. A little hair of the dog could be had at the outdoor bar of this mansion hotel by the ocean. *No, no,* the thoughts of a cool glass of wine caused her temples to twitch. Not her usual reaction to that idea. *Better turn right and go the longer route.* The narrow path from start to finish was three and a half miles long. Most of the trail was paved but if she made it far enough she knew the pavement would give way to a dirt path then to a scramble over large, sometimes slippery, rocks.

Maddie nodded a friendly greeting to some visitors admiring the view of the ocean framed by the abundant thorny thickets of beach plum roses. As she approached The Breakers, the largest of the mansions open to the public, she thought of Winston. He had mentioned the Gilded Age, a time when the extremely wealthy, including his family, had built these stone palaces as monuments to their egos, creating tangible foundations for their legacies.

Cliff Walk passed before sixty-four private residences. Protective iron fences, often with a hedgerow as an added buffer, kept visitors on the path at a respectable distance. Her romantic mind churned as she wondered if Winston was like one of these Gilded Age manors; *keeping his distance from me with a virtual emotional wall.* Although he seemed engaged in their conversations, and she enjoyed spending time with him, she still did not feel connected to him. Perhaps it was the exclusive setting he was brought up in. She suspected he did not subscribe to the idea that character is something you build, not something you are born with, and perhaps his upbringing might make it very difficult for him to share his inner fears and hopes. *Or maybe it's me? I haven't been on the dating circuit for a few years. Maybe I'm the one putting up a fence? I should have a fence around me, probably some padded walls too. I remember being spontaneous and carefree. I think I just need to*--Maddie's internal musings were brought to a halt by a loud plea.

"Excuse me!"

She turned to face a small cluster of ladies and a round-faced woman calling to her.

"Would you please take our picture with the Tea House?"

"Of course," Maddie smiled and took the camera.

The woman who seemed in charge barked through an internal megaphone. "This is where Mrs. Vanderbilt-Belmont held suffragette meetings! Come on girls, get together!" With a wave of her wobbly, wing-like arm the leader directed her flock to stand near the side of the Walk's tunnel which ran underneath a Chinese pagoda. Maddie handed the camera back.

"Thanks so much, dear. Girls, we'll get off the Walk up ahead and take a proper tour of The Marble House and this pagoda Tea House! Have a good day, dear."

Maddie wasn't sure if the woman was naturally shrill or if the remnants of her hangover were making her overly sensitive. Either way, she decided to stop here and take a break. She looked up at the tourists milling about the Marble House's extensive lawn as they clicked photos of the unique Tea House above Cliff Walk at the edge of the ocean. Its jade and red colors complemented the Asian architecture, so different from the adjacent Greek revival Marble House. *Different cultures, diverse designs, together as a landmark property. Would Winston and I really be able to combine our distinct backgrounds into one relationship? Why the hell am I worried about a relationship? I know at this point we're just friends.*

Right on time, the afternoon prevailing wind rose up to swirl her hair from her face and cool the back of her neck, encouraging her to forge on. The air tasted of summer. She filled her nostrils with the salty smell of the sea mixed with the earthy, sweet scent of seaweed clinging to the craggy rocks below. In the distance, she could just make out the turn where the path began its downward slope and changed from safe cement to a potentially dangerous dance over rugged riprap. Focusing on her footing would help to clear her mind. She realized her headache had subsided and she was ready to embrace the challenge.

# EIGHT

**P**ing. The elevator door opened on the fourth floor. Sarah Byron pulled open the glass door in front of her and stepped into Spinnaker Ventures. Ken kept his eyes on his computer screen as she approached his oversized oak desk.

"Congratulations," Sarah said as she plopped a Forbes magazine down on top of Ken's keyboard. "Your friend's company made the cover of the magazine but your mail made it down to my office again."

Ken looked at the magazine's bent pages knowing she had read the article. *Nosy freakin' bitch*, he thought. "And how do you know he's my friend, Sarah?"

"Because I've seen you two leaving the building at lunchtime when I'm heading out."

Ken wanted to smack the smart-ass smirk right off her pasty freckled face. *It figures this busy-body bitch wouldn't miss a trick.*

"Besides, he mentions you, and Spinnaker Ventures, as his source of initial capital in the story."

"So you read my mail, Sarah?" Ken's icy stare made Sarah look a whole lot less sure of herself.

"Well, it's just that it came to my office, and I didn't realize it was your company's mail until I read the back label."

"You work for a tee shirt company, Sarah. Why the hell would your company be receiving Forbes magazine in the first place? Didn't it dawn on you this might be a mistake? Don't you remember the new mail guy sometimes gets confused between the third and fourth floors of this building and mixes up our mail?"

Ken's sharp retort caused Sarah to take a step backward, her mouth fell agape and her eyes opened wide. Ken continued to glare at her for another few seconds, to be sure she got the message. Then he turned back to his computer screen. "Thanks for the mail, Sarah, you know the way out."

Sarah burst into tears in the elevator; thinking, *all I wanted to do was flirt a little, maybe get an introduction to his cute friend. Gosh, how could such an attractive man on the outside be so ugly on the inside?*

Ken picked up the magazine and thumbed through to the article on Jared Diamond. The piece briefly touched on the fact Ken and Jared had met in college. The truth was they had actually met in Tuscany. Ken was staying at his parents' home there for the summer and Jared was on a study abroad program. They were the only two English speaking people at a small café and were astounded when they realized they were both entering their sophomore year at Tufts University. Ken was a finance major and Jared was in the engineering program. They spent the summer immersed in Tuscan culture; food, wine, hiking, concerts. Once they returned to school in the fall they were almost inseparable. Ken knew with computers Jared was a visionary; and that his programming skills would lead to something big. However, he also knew with business Jared was pretty much an idiot. After college Ken's uncle set him up with the funds to create his venture capital company, Spinnaker Ventures. The first startup company Ken invested in belonged to Jared -- Diamond Enterprises. It took six years but now that investment had paid off big time. Jared had written a computer application which he had sold to the military and was now being used at Raytheon Integrated Defense Systems in Newport. The program was very successful and had made Jared millions. It also landed him on the covers of leading industry and money magazines. The article indicated this was just the tip of the iceberg as the computer application had potential to expand to the civilian market.

Ken closed the magazine and looked at the cover photo. Even when posed, Jared's smile had a warm, boyish quality that drew you in.

*Not the picture of Jared I would've picked,* he thought.

# NINE

Maddie dug into the pocket of her jeans trying to extract the ringing cell phone as she stepped inside her house. It was Winston.

"Hello, Madison. What are you up to?"

"I just got back from a long, head-clearing stroll along Cliff Walk."

"Oh, why did you need to clear your head? Are you okay, Madison?"

"Yes, I'm fine. I mean nothing's bothering me." Prompting her to think, *actually, a lot seems to be bothering me including worrying about us.* Instead, she continued, "It was just a late Friday night with a few too many drinks with my friend Kelly."

"I remember you telling me about Kelly. Was her fiancé there too?"

"No, no boys allowed. It was just a girls' night to catch up."

"No boys, really?" Winston's tone was not accusatory, but more amused.

"No boys all night, Winston, I would let you know." Maddie smiled to herself. She welcomed his concern but she was especially pleased with the indication it would be difficult to make a man like him jealous. After Joe, the last thing she wanted to see was the green-eyed monster again. And he was a monster.

"So, what's going on with you, Mr. Cooper?"

"Well, I called to see if you would like to join me at the New York Yacht Club tomorrow, around seven p.m. for dinner?"

"You want to go to New York for dinner?"

Winston chuckled. "No," he said. "The club has a Newport location."

"I had no idea."

Maddie had never been on a boat, let alone set foot in a yacht club. "Let me check…Sunday… yes, I'm clear. Do you want to meet at my house for a drink first?"

"Actually, I will be on my way back from one of my charity events in Boston. So it would be better to meet at Harbour Court."

"Wait, where is Harbour Court?"

Winston laughed again. "Sorry, I realize this must sound confusing. Estates here in Newport have names."

He didn't sound condescending, so she tried not to sound annoyed. "I know that, Winston, I live on one."

"Well, Harbour Court is the name of the house which used to belong to John Nicholas Brown. After he died, the Club purchased Harbour Court. So, we now have a waterfront location, as well as the New York City location."

"Well, I guess it's just another little bit of history I'll get to explore. I look forward to seeing you there at seven."

"You've made my day, Madison. See you then."

Maddie made a mental note to remember to ask Winston about his charitable work. *Is it possible to be handsome, rich, caring and compassionate? Well, Prince William exists*, she mused, *so why not Winston?* Maddie wanted to think the best of him, but if Winston was everything she believed...*why doesn't he have a girlfriend?* She made another mental note to ask about that too.

She researched the New York Yacht Club at Harbour Court on her computer. She had no inkling about this club, or where it was located, and she sure as heck hoped she didn't need a secret hand-shake to get in.

# TEN

Winston's mind drifted back to the day he met Madison Marcelle at the law office. He had arrived for his monthly meeting with the partners to go over the trusts when he spotted the most vulnerable looking girl he had ever seen. She was so beautiful and seemed so nervous; sitting on that big leather couch, looking down, picking at her fingernails, never mind that he was not used to seeing anyone under the age of fifty in that office, he was absolutely intrigued. The brief chat he had with her left him yearning for more. He told the partners he didn't care about rules, he needed to have her cell phone number.

"Hello, son."

Winston looked up from the Wall Street Journal lying across his lap.

"Am I interrupting your reading?"

"No, not all, Father."

The tight-fitting white polo shirt and tennis shorts James Cooper wore were swirled with sweat.

"How was your match?" Winston asked.

James shook his head, his strong, toned physique belied his chronological age of sixty-five. "That damn Skipper Johnson bested me."

"Were you here on our court?"

33

"No, no we were over at the Tennis Hall of Fame. I just don't do as well when we play on those grass courts."

Gargoyles carved into a black walnut sideboard oversaw James as he removed the lid from a gleaming, silver bucket, scooped out a handful of ice and added,

"But I'll get a chance to redeem myself next week. So are you working on getting me a daughter-in-law?" prodded James.

"As a matter of fact, I am. Remember the girl I told you about from Anderson and Anderson?"

"Yes, the nurse. Inherited Randall Whitmore's money. She's young, right, childbearing age?" his father commented holding a cold, dripping monogrammed bar towel up to his neck.

"Yes, Father, Madison is twenty-six, smart, funny-"

"And beautiful, I did a little investigating," interrupted James.

"Yes, very beautiful and not a gold digger."

"Good," approved his father, "but not as important at this point. I need a grandson even if I have to pay her off."

"Father, might I remind you that you were thirty-five when I was born and I am just over the mark of thirty."

James fished his hand back into the ice bucket and popped a cube into his mouth. He stood shoulder to shoulder with his son and slapped a large hand on Winston's back. "Yes, but I was married to your mother at thirty and you are my one and only child. As it turned out it took more time than we thought to have you. Remember that, even the best plans should have a backup plan, son."

"So, what was your backup plan if you didn't have me?" Winston jeered.

James tilted his head, looked Winston in the eye and deadpanned, "Cloning. Now listen to me, if Madison is as she seems you need to get serious about her and move this along. We don't know how long I will be around."

Winston stepped aside and turned to face his father with an incredulous look. "Father, you play tennis every week, you swim daily, you still sail the boat around. Hell, you're in better shape than most men half your age!"

"You just never know, Winston. See those dogs?" James pointed up to a hefty, gold-framed oil painting of an English hunt scene. "That's like your cousins sniffing around, waiting to pull, tear, attack and take away my money, our money."

"Father I know you're concerned. I understand this is about our family legacy. I will do whatever it takes to make this happen."

His father nodded his head and urged, "Soon."

"Yes, as I started to tell you earlier, I am meeting Madison tomorrow at Harbour Court."

"Brilliant!" exclaimed his father. "Now will you be joining your mother and me for dinner tonight or do you have big Saturday night plans?"

"No, no plans. That would be fine. Usual time, Father?"

"Yes, I will have your mother let Cook know. Perhaps we could have Madison join us too?" James gave Winston a hopeful look.

"Father, I promise I will work things out with Madison, but I can't scare her off, patience, please."

"Well, your mother will be happy to hear you at least have a serious relationship in your life. I'll see you at 6:00 p.m. sharp, son."

Winston smiled at his father. "Yes sir, 6:00 p.m. sharp." His father turned and left the library.

Winston closed the heavy doors of the mahogany-paneled library. He walked back over to the oil painting depicting the hunt scene, admired it for a second then slid it to the side; revealing a wall safe. He typed in the code, reached inside and retrieved a stack of papers. He scanned through the document and re-read the lines he had almost memorized. *Meeting Madison was a stroke of serendipity, perfect timing. A beautiful young girl with no baggage, no ex-husbands, no children yet, no family ties, and her own money to top it off. She's vulnerable and a little cautious. I can work with that*, he thought. He closed the painting back over the safe, poured three fingers of Scotch into a cut crystal glass and sank into a leather club chair. He closed his eyes, he needed to think.

# ELEVEN

"So, do you want moo shi or pad Thai tonight?"

Jared looked up from his desk to see Ken waving a paper menu at him. "Sorry, Ken, not tonight. I've got a YPO thing to go to."

"YPO?"

"Yeah, it's this invitation-only business group, stands for Young Presidents Organization. It's good for networking, business advice, you know."

"I do know, that's why I thought you had me around."

"And I am grateful to you for coming to my office to check over the books and keep the business stuff running. But it doesn't hurt to branch out and go to this type of event."

"So, I guess I'll just stay at your office, all by myself, and slave over the books alone and hungry."

Jared walked over to Ken and gave him a placating head tip. "You know I would much rather hang out with you and eat take-out than to try to elbow my way into a room full of egos. But I made a commitment to go."

"Well, remember, I made a commitment to go too. I am going to be out of the country on Monday," Ken reminded Jared.

Jared was now milling about his office looking for Bret Tolim's address, where the event was being held.

"Oh, right. You did tell me you would be away. Well, I think you have access to whatever you need for tonight."

"What about that new accountant? Can I get into his computer too?" asked Ken.

"Yeah, that would be Shane." Jared went back to his desk and clicked a few keystrokes on his computer. "Here you go, that's Shane's password and these are the codes for the other two accountants in case you forgot them."

"I don't forget; for example, I don't forget when I have plans to spend the evening with a friend," Ken sneered.

Jared put his arm around Ken's shoulders. "Come on, you know I'm no good at working out the numbers. Besides, every time we do this you always do all the work and I end up eating more than my share of whatever we've ordered. Just make sure we're still making money, everyone is being paid and I will see you when you get back in town."

"Yes sir, you're the boss."

Jared returned Ken's smirk and pointed a finger at him. "And don't you forget it. Now, give me something besides financial advice. Do I need to change this shirt or will it do for business casual?"

Ken pulled open the closet where Jared kept a variety of extra clothes. Long hours, often at unusual times, dictated that Jared's office be his second home. Ken looked Jared over and shook his head. "A polo shirt is too casual. You need one of your button-downs."

Ken watched Jared strip off his top then handed him a striped, long-sleeve dress shirt. "This is why you need me."

Jared smiled at Ken's pointed remark.

"And don't you forget it!" Ken called as Jared headed out the door.

# TWELVE

Maddie opened her closet and picked through dresses on the rack. *Let's see, something nautical, this one is definitely not classy enough, what's back here?* She spied a box half hidden under a long wool coat. She yanked it out into the room and pulled it open, *oh crap, that's why I didn't unpack this.* She reached in and carefully raised a photo of Joe. *Damn you, Joe. I loved you so much, too much.* Hot tears stung the corners of her eyes for a few seconds before the ache turned to anger.

Seeing Joe writhing on top of their landlady was the catalyst that hurled her out of the relationship. But the damage her fiancé had caused started long before she witnessed him cheating on her.

At first, it worked. She had spent many years without a father and being with Joe was a comfort. He was strong, and not just physically. He was also confident. He would fix her car, help her balance her checkbook, encourage her to save money, call to make sure she made it to the hospital for her shift. She liked having him take care of her. He invited her to hang out with all of his friends. He involved her in his activities. He even picked out the movies they watched. He was so decisive, and her job at the hospital was so stressful. It was simple to let him take over the reins of their personal life.

Over time, all her friends but Kelly dropped away as Joe made it clear he did not like them. It was easier to hang out with the guys than to get into another fight about her 'stupid friends.'

She had worked for Mr. Whitmore for two months before she mustered the courage to tell Joe she had left the hospital and started a new job. The fight was inevitable, but at least she could stand by her claim that the position with Mr. Whitmore was working out.

The hurt Joe had caused Maddie went beyond his physical pushing and shoving. It was the emotional betrayal and self-doubt he inflicted which really wounded her. Only after she moved out of his apartment did she realize what used to seem like a caring concern for her was actually domineering control over her.

*You betrayed my complete trust, Joe! But that's the problem, isn't it? I trusted you and stopped trusting myself. I let you make all the decisions and now I talk to myself and question my own choices. Mr. Whitmore reminded me I am smart, and I can be strong. But now that he's gone, I don't feel very strong. Mr. Whitmore...*

Maddie stood up, walked to an antique chest of drawers and pulled out a small envelope. Jeff Shorey had given it to her at the law office. Although she had read it before, right now it felt like Mr. Whitmore was speaking in her ear. She needed to re-visit his words. She opened it and re-read the craggy writing.

*My dear girl Maddie,*

*I know you love to learn. Life will continue teaching you lessons. Even when they are hard, you must find meaning in them. I hope that you will keep learning about life but most importantly you will learn about yourself.*

*With Love,*

*RW*

41

# THIRTEEN

"Hey, Jared! Glad you could make it."

The invitation to this enclave of capitalists extended only to the presidents and CEOs of companies. Spouses were not allowed at the meetings, but sometimes they would show up and gather about in another part of the host's home.

"Thanks, Bret. Is your wife here?" Jared asked.

"No, she arranged for a spouse outing so we don't have to meet behind closed doors. Let's grab a drink at the bar and then I have a couple people I want you to meet."

Jared looked around Bret's family room, filled with well-groomed men. Jared had worked with some business savvy women but sadly, as evidenced by this group, Captains of Industry was still a male-dominated group.

"Jared, I want you to meet-"

"Charlie Mara!" Jared finished Bret's introduction as Charlie and Jared clasped hands and beamed.

"You two know each other I take it?" Bret commented.

"Yeah, Jared and I went to high school together."

Bret smiled and stepped back. "I'll let you guys grab some drinks and get caught up. The program starts in about half an hour."

"So, I know what you've been up to Jared; between interviews and every money magazine keeping tabs on you it's pretty hard not to," Charlie said with a smile.

"Yeah, things are going pretty well. So, Charlie, what are you doing these days?"

"I have my own accounting firm. I do audit work, handle some individual accounts and some consulting. Most of the stuff I do is with small to mid-size companies, like yours. Who are you using as an auditor?"

"I got a friend of mine, invested in the company early, he helped me get the business end set up. He comes in and helps out, you know, guides my in-house accounting people, checks over the books."

"That's fine for everyday stuff but from what I've read, your company's growing, Jared. You really need to have an independent auditor, not just a friend who helps out. It's standard business practice for a company your size. Correct me if I'm wrong, I heard on CNBC you might be planning an IPO."

"Yeah, I don't handle the business stuff, Charlie, but the applications I'm developing now could very well expand into the civilian market. I'm not sure about taking the company public yet but it certainly could be a reality."

"You know Jared, I'd be more than happy to come by your office and look things over. No charge. See if I can help you out."

"That would be great but my business guy, Ken Tate, will be out of the country starting this Monday. Honestly, I don't know how much help I can be on my own."

Charlie held up his hand like a cop stopping traffic. "Do you know how to access your accounts?"

"I do."

"No problem then, as long as you can get me to the information I can start a review. I could even come by tomorrow."

"Sure, if you don't mind working on a Sunday, Charlie. I'm free all day. I'll meet you there and try to get you everything you need."

"Sounds good. Let's go hit the bar before the program starts here."

Jared thought briefly about texting Ken to let him know he and Charlie would be at the office tomorrow but dismissed the idea. *No need to bother Ken, he's heading away on Monday. Charlie knows what he's doing and it wouldn't kill me to get involved with the business end of my own company instead of relying on Ken all the time,* he thought.

# FOURTEEN

Maddie left for the New York Yacht Club early. Very early. Once, she would not have shied away from a new experience but heading solo to a private club made her a bit anxious; lately, it seemed most things made her anxious. *Unbelievable*, she thought as she looked from the GPS to the familiar road ahead. *I've driven this road a thousand times and never knew this was the club.*

A barely noticeable small bronze plaque, half covered with ivy, was posted on a privacy wall denoting the French style chateau beyond was the NYYC. She angled her car into the tapered driveway which opened up to large gravel parking areas surrounded by lush hillside gardens. *Good thing I don't like wearing heels,* she thought as she finished her hike from the lower parking lot and arrived at a circular drive on top of the hill. Just beyond the fountain in the center of the loop was the main entrance. She hung back a moment and watched an older couple slowly emerge from a classic Jaguar then push open the enormous carved wood doors and disappear. She stood back as the Jaguar whisked past her down to the parking lot. The grin on the valet's face made her think of the movie *Ferris Buehler's Day Off*.

The confidence she had mustered to proceed inside was swept away with the closing of the door behind her. She had barely taken in the foyer when a reedy man, about her age, dressed in a navy-blue suit with a pink silk handkerchief poking out of his chest pocket approached her with raised eyebrows and asked if he could help her. She felt her right hand reach under the nails of her left hand, then reminded herself she was an invited visitor and deserved to be here as much as anyone else. She pulled her posture up a little higher and met his eye. "Yes, I'm a guest of Winston Cooper. He is meeting me here."

His officious expression immediately changed and he became a smiling sycophant. "Oh, Yes! Mr. Cooper! Welcome to the Club, Miss—?"

"Marcelle. Madison Marcelle."

"Welcome Miss Marcelle. Please follow me." Maddie fell in line behind him. She allowed her eyes to wander up the walnut wainscoted walls, past large oil paintings of ships, to the intricate coffered ceiling. It didn't matter how much money she had inherited, she was still impressed every time she entered one of these mammoth old mansions in Newport.

The salon was warm inside from sunlight pouring in through large, high set windows behind the bar. French doors flanked the room offering spectacular water views. Maddie stepped through a glass door onto a stone patio set as if it were the apex of a pyramid; as the lawn just beyond pitched steeply down to the water and the club's docks. She ventured past a few umbrella-covered tables and settled into one of the inviting Adirondack chairs, lined in a row, overlooking Brenton Cove, the Pell-Newport Bridge and the boat filled harbor.

"It looks like you could use a drink as much as I could use another one."

Maddie shielded her eyes from the late day sun and looked up toward the cheerful voice matched by an engaging smile. "Been a long day has it?" she commented.

"Well, let's just say wading through numbers and looking over accounts left me out of my element at my own office."

Maddie cocked her head to the side and took in the attractive man standing over her chair. *Is this guy flirting with me? Probably not. He's cute, must have a girlfriend. Probably just being friendly. No one else sitting out here. What is wrong with me? We're at a private club, he's not going to kill me.* She decided there was no harm in continuing the conversation. "Working on a Sunday?"

"My business knows no day of the week."

"And what is your business?"

"Diamond Enterprises, it's a computer business." Jared thrust his hand down toward Maddie's face. "Hi. I'm Jared Diamond. I create computer applications."

"Nice to meet you, Jared, my name is Madison, Maddie, Marcelle and I used to be a nurse."

A server arrived, dressed in a white polo shirt emblazoned with the New York Yacht Club's navy flag, red cross, and white star insignia. "May I take your order?"

Maddie ordered a chardonnay. Jared ordered another gin and tonic and gave the server his account number.

He relaxed into an Adirondack chair next to Maddie's and asked, "So, are you a member here?"

Maddie gave him a nervous smile and quickly rambled, "No, not a member. I'm actually new to money, but I'm meeting a friend here. A date. And he's a member."

Jared found her nervousness to be disarming. This girl wasn't like the usual suspects hanging out at the club. *Definitely worth the risk to pry about the date situation*, he thought. "I'm fairly new to money too, I mean I didn't grow up with a lot of it, but now that I've earned some I'm enjoying it."

As the conversation continued Maddie was struck by Jared's unpretentious attitude. His clever wit and irreverent observations of their surroundings had her laughing and feeling like a spy performing reconnaissance on foreign, opulent terrain.

"Maddie, I must tell you, I find you quite refreshing and easy to talk to. So how serious is this date of yours?"

Maddie's eyes opened wide. She was completely taken aback by this sudden turn in dialogue.

"I'm sorry that was rude," Jared apologized and looked down into his glass. "It's just that it's been a long time since I've met anyone as interesting, down to earth, funny and pretty as you. I apologize if I offended you and I wish you the best with your boyfriend." Jared rose from his chair but Maddie caught his arm.

"He's not my boyfriend," she blurted out.

Jared couldn't suppress the stunned smile that came over his face.

Maddie was just as surprised at her own impulsiveness. But the wine had relaxed her and she had enjoyed her talk with Jared way too much. She didn't want it to end yet, but she also realized she needed to be clear about her dating situation. "I mean, I am dating Winston but we're not exclusive."

"So, Maddie, if you were to give me your phone number and I were to call you, you would consider continuing our conversation?"

Maddie smiled. She could hear Kelly inside her head telling her to be open to meeting new men. Jared whipped out his phone and tapped in the numbers. He had just set his phone on the arm of his chair when a tall shadow appeared next to Maddie.

"Hello, Madison." Winston Cooper bent down and gave Maddie a kiss on the cheek then stretched his hand out, giving a self-introduction to Jared.

Jared stood up, gripped Winston's hand firmly, and returned the pleasantry. However, much to Maddie's dismay, the exchange did not end there.

The two men were clearly sizing each other up. *Oh, crap,* thought Maddie *they look like a couple of grizzly bears, all puffed up, circling each other, growling and jabbing.* Except their jabs were verbal.

Jared dropped his hand but continued to look Winston in the eye as he silently assessed him. *Damn, I'm no slouch but this guy is handsome. For cripes sake, he even has a chin dimple! I'm six foot, so is he. Soft hands, wouldn't do well in a street fight. Probably better suited to a round of fencing.*

49

"So good to meet you, Jared. Thanks for taking care of Madison before I got here. I didn't realize I was running late," Winston stated as he took in his potential competition. *Good looking. About my height and age. He looks athletic, but so am I.*

"Oh, you weren't late," Maddie jumped in. "I got here early."

Winston turned to her and nodded dismissively, he wasn't done with Jared yet. "So I take it you're a member here. Where do you keep your boat?"

Jared pointed across the harbor. "Right over there at my dock in Jamestown."

Throws and shots about houses and boats continued to fly. Maddie was unsure how to play referee.

"You look familiar, Jared. Did I play lacrosse or football with you at Harvard?" Winston's eyes narrowed thinking he might have Jared backed into a corner, he continued. "Of course, if it was football you might remember me. I was the quarterback."

"No, I was never a lacrosse or football player. Baseball was always my thing, pitcher, from little league through college. And I went to Tufts, not Harvard," Jared said with a smile, *time to take Winston down.* "Maybe you recognize me from the cover of Forbes magazine? I was just named the top entrepreneur to watch for my computer company, Diamond Enterprises. What line of work are you in?"

"I'm involved in a lot of philanthropic work," Winston punched back.

*That's it!* Maddie couldn't take the macho dance any longer. "Jared, thank you so much for the drinks. I believe Winston and I have a reservation for dinner inside."

Winston turned and gave Maddie a pacifying smile, then turned back to Jared, his smile slowly pushing the corners of his mouth even higher. *I win!* "Please, allow me to put your drinks on my tab."

But Jared insisted, "No, no I'm a gentleman and it was my pleasure to meet you both, besides I've already signed for it on my account."

"Alright, have a good evening." Winston took Maddie by the arm and steered her back towards the French doors.

As Jared watched Maddie and Winston disappear inside his phone buzzed. "Hi, Charlie. Missing money? Money transfers, no I haven't moved any money. Okay. Okay. Yes, keep digging and let me know what you find. I'll do some investigating on my end too. And Charlie, let's just keep this between us for now." Jared hung up. He could feel his blood pressure rising. He punched numbers into his phone. It was not a call he wanted to make, it was a call he needed to make.

# FIFTEEN

"Hello, handsome. I thought you weren't going to call me 'til mid-week? It's only Sunday. I just saw you."

"I know," he said to the man on the other end of the line, "but I need to see you, I need to be with you right now."

"Yes sir, I'm all yours tonight."

# SIXTEEN

"The London Exchange has been open for over five hours and I still haven't received confirmation of my order. I don't give a crap if your wife is sick, Monty," James Cooper barked into the Bluetooth attached to his ear as he fished around the cavernous athletic gear room. "If you don't execute my sell order in the next five minutes you'll wish your only problem was your wife!"

James continued to pull tennis racquets down from shelves and rifle through duffle bags on the bench below.

"Where the hell is it? Sally, Sally get in here. Jesus, woman, are you deaf?" James shouted as he turned towards a door that led to the kitchen.

Sally entered with a sheepish smile on her face. "I'm here, Mr. Cooper."

"Finally. What did you do with my lucky racquet? I'm playing Johnson this morning and I need it."

"Would it be the Wilson BLX?"

In two long steps James Cooper was towering over Sally's face, his voice escalated to a bellow, "Of course it's the Wilson BLX, you know it's my lucky racquet and you know that you moved it!"

Sally calmly replied, "I did not move your lucky racquet, Mr. Cooper."

James's left hand reached around to engulf Sally's right buttock. "Damn it Sally you know I enjoy spending time with your sweet ass, but you can't keep screwing with my stuff."

Sally looked up and locked eyes with James as she steadily stated, "I too enjoy our time together. I have never screwed with your stuff and I didn't touch your lucky racquet. If you want to know where it is, go ask your wife. I saw her put it in her tennis bag yesterday."

James squeezed her lower cheek hard then gave her full backside a sharp smack as he sighed. "Well, I guess I'll have to go track her down."

Sally crumpled her mouth and muttered, "If she just paid attention to the system I set up out here for the two of you we wouldn't have this problem."

James snatched up Sally's wrist and hissed, "Never, ever, speak of my wife in that tone again or it will be the last thing you say. Understand?"

Sally swallowed hard as she nodded her head up and down. "Yes sir. Sorry sir."

James dropped her wrist. Sally scurried back toward the door that adjoined the kitchen to the athletic gear room, rubbing her red, sore wrist.

~~~~~~~~

The door to the bedroom burst open as James strode into his wife's dressing room. "Lolly darling, I've been looking everywhere for you."

Lolly Barrows-Cooper looked at James through her vanity mirror, carefully set her hairbrush down and turned to face her husband. "Are you alright, my love? You look harried."

Despite having lived more than thirty years in the United States, the sixty-year-old Lolly had retained her British accent. James swept down and gave his wife a gentle kiss on top of her smooth, blonde hair.

"Just getting ready for my match against Skipper Johnson and noticed my lucky racquet is missing from the gear room."

"Oh, I didn't even know you had a lucky racquet, love," Lolly answered with surprise. "Why don't you check with Sally? She's good at making sure things get put away in there." Wealth and privilege were all Lolly had ever known which made it hard to tell if she was oblivious to other people's problems, or just too selfish to care.

"Yes, Darling, it is part of her job so I checked with her and she seems to think you had it yesterday in your tennis bag."

Lolly giggled. "Silly me. I might have, love. You know me, I just grab and go."

James gave her a placating smile. "Yes, Darling, I know. Now, where do you think you might have put your bag, dear?" James tenderly guided Lolly by the elbow as she rose from a tufted bench.

James smiled down at her, transfixed by her impossibly crystal blue eyes. He had married Lolly to give his estate a financial transfusion. Her assets had provided funds for him to invest, thus boosting their fortune back into the billions. Over time he had grown to love his wife. He loved the way she glided through life, always upbeat, always beautiful, always supportive of him, and always aloof to his darker moods and desires.

Lolly tapped a finger on her rosy lips. "Let's see, after my match yesterday – oh, I came straight up to shower. I must have set the bag in here."

She walked from the vanity area into an adjacent room that held her vast collection of shoes, clothes, and jewels. James followed as she wandered in front of him poking at color-coded, dangling garments and peeking beneath them. Lolly seemed distracted by an emerald green dress. "This color looks so nice with my eyes. Don't you agree, James?"

"You look beautiful in all colors, darling. Perhaps you left it by the laundry room for Sally or Mary to take care of? I'll go out and see."

"Of course! That's exactly where I left it. James, you are truly the smartest man I have ever known. What would I do without you?"

James kissed his wife on the cheek. "Fortunately, darling, you will never need to answer that question. I will see you tonight for dinner."

Lolly embraced James, stroking his thick salt and pepper hair away from his forehead. "Yes, my love, I will be anxious to hear all about your match with Skipper and who was lunching at the club. Good luck."

Lolly ran a perfectly manicured finger along a groove etched into the mahogany stair rail as she wound her way down to the first floor of her Newport castle. She peered through a leaded glass window in her private office and watched the waves break on the rocks before turning her attention to the task at hand. *Time to address invitations,* she thought.

She pulled her 'bible' from a shelf. A notebook of names, dates, events, and notes detailing behaviors. This 'bible' contained crucial information for her to consult before addressing invitations to the Flowers in the Moonlight Ball. After all, it was the signature event of the social season.

Her involvement in charity work did not stem from empathy for the cause. It was simply what she was raised to do. Her real joy came from knowing she was at the top of the social ladder. The Flowers in the Moonlight Ball would be another opportunity to revel in the power of either giving a leg up to social climbers who pleased her or casting down ones who did not.

# SEVENTEEN

Cosimo had to honor his uncle's wishes with Bob, but it took every fiber of his being to not put the spoiled little prick in the ground. Every time he thought he had just cause to get rid of him, that damn cockroach would somehow manage to convince people, himself included, that he was worth keeping around. He had no respect for a thirty-two-year-old man whose only real skill in life was essentially begging. Cosimo DeCastellerri was old school. He believed you needed to earn a seat at the table. Bob was barely qualified to sit with the kids.

*Sponging off his mother's ability to spread her legs and keep my uncle happy all those years is not something a true man would be proud of,* Cosimo thought. He rubbed his eyes with his thick fingers, the more he thought about the freakin' cockroach the angrier he got. He needed to get that idiot off his mind. He had bigger fish to fry.

"Mikey!" Cosimo shouted out.

Cosimo's guard stood up and hulked around the desk to face Mr. D.

"Make me a cappuccino," Cosimo demanded.

# EIGHTEEN

Like brushing her teeth, part of Maddie's daily routine now included either texting or calling Winston. Today's conversation would not be so natural. She certainly didn't regret giving her number to Jared but after her experience with Joe, she needed Winston to know how important honesty and trust were to her. She had decided to explain her past with Joe to Winston. She wanted to be upfront about keeping the door open and dating other men, for now. She hoped Winston would understand and at a minimum they could stay friends, but she truly hoped they could move forward and see if they could be something more.

Maddie hung up from the call as a few tears of relief seeped from her eyes. Winston had been so kind, he wasn't ready to give up on her yet.

~~~~~~~~

"Shit!" Winston flung his cell phone onto a bench along the side of his tennis court. Jared Diamond had just become a complication.

"Well you're in a foul mood," James Cooper commented to his son as he picked up his racquet.

"Yes, it seems a kink has developed in my plan to move forward with your potential daughter-in-law."

James eyed Winston sternly. "Son, haven't I taught you to have a backup plan?"

Winston rolled his head to the side and sighed, "Yes, Father."

"But sometimes, son, a good plan just needs to," James tossed a tennis ball high into the air and tracked it with his eyes, "have the kink knocked out." His powerful swat smashed the ball into the next court.

# NINETEEN

Ken shook the morning dew off his Ferragamo shoes as he dipped into his BMW. His flight didn't leave for another three hours but he didn't want to get caught in Monday traffic through Boston.

Ken stretched his legs and looked up, ready for his favorite in-flight entertainment-- watching the frustration build on the faces of the people trying to squeeze past him through the aisle on their way to coach. He couldn't even remember what it was like to fold up your legs and jam into the seats back there, as the one and only time he had not flown first class was when he was about eighteen and nothing else was available.

~~~~~~~

A balmy breeze rippled through the trees as he strolled up to the bank. Ken stared patiently at a young, bucktoothed customer service girl as she typed information into her computer and set up his new account. He studied her face, trying not to grimace. *Ugly and slow,* he thought.

"Just a few more minutes Mr. Tate," the girl drawled out.

*Stupid girl.* His lips drew across into a tight line that passed as a smile as he lied. "Take your time."

# TWENTY

B ob spoke into his cell phone as he drove away from Newport along Indian Avenue, past enormous shingle style and brick homes.

"Tell Mr. D that I will have his money tomorrow morning. I'm going to pick it up tonight. Right, by 10 a.m. I will be on The Hill in his office. Bye."

He had begged, he had promised, he had pleaded, he had practically prostrated himself on the floor and Bob had managed to convince Cosimo to give him a seventy-two-hour extension on the money he owed.

He pulled his new Mustang around a circular driveway and parked his car. Bob opened his glove box, removed three Jack Daniels nips and sucked them all down to get ready for the pick-up. This was not the first time, hell not even the second time he had come here for money.

He admired the ornately carved wood pediment over the doorway for a moment before he rang the bell of the stately brick, Federal style home.

Mrs. Vanderbeck opened the door. Her eyes slowly moved from Bob's slick, black hair down to his shoes. When her gaze met with his again, a smirk spread across her face. "Please come in," she invited.

Mrs. Vanderbeck turned and he followed this tall, slender woman with perfect posture inside to a well-appointed parlor.

"What do you think of my latest acquisition?" she asked and gestured to a canvas hanging over a fireplace.

Bob tilted his head to the right, the wavy dark lines and chunks of paint reminded him of something his grandmother's cat used to cough up. Bob shrugged his shoulders. "I'm not sure what it's supposed to be."

Mrs. Vanderbeck snickered. "It's contemporary art. It's an abstract representation of this era's struggle to prop up the waning middle class and the wide disparity forming between the very wealthy and the very poor."

Bob's mind reeled at how she even came to that interpretation. "Wow. I was way off."

Mrs. Vanderbeck gave Bob a condescending grin. "Drink?" she asked.

"Ah, yeah, you got, ah, whiskey?"

Mrs. Vanderbeck smiled. "Ice?"

"No, no thanks." Bob didn't want to dilute his liquid courage.

Mrs. Vanderbeck sauntered back to where Bob was still standing, drink in one hand, manila envelope in the other. Bob took the glass and reached for the envelope. Mrs. Vanderbeck snatched it up over her head.

"Tisk, tisk, just wanted to show you I included some extra, since you did such a good job last time." She turned and glided back to the bar, her lavender silk robe billowing out behind her. She propped the envelope up against a bottle of vodka then took a seat on a long, green brocade couch. "Please, join me."

Bob downed his whiskey in two gulps then slowly moved toward the couch. Mrs. Vanderbeck ran a hand through her trim silver and white hair. As he approached, she unfastened the sash around her robe. He was standing over her now. She allowed her garment to slide from her shoulders. Bob looked at the pale, crepe skin draped over her form, like a tissue you had stored in your pocket then tried to smooth out before using—soft, but not what it once was. Bob held her face and gave her an almost dry kiss.

"Mmm. That's nice," she remarked, "but you know where I want to be kissed."

Bob took a deep breath then lowered his body down the couch.

~~~~~~~

The encounter with his cougar with cash had paid off. The money in the envelope covered his debt to Mr. D and then some. Now he needed to feel young and very numb. He was on his way to the clubs in Newport to use the bonus money he had just earned.

# TWENTY-ONE

Kelly and Maddie arrived while the band still was setting up, so they were able to score a couple seats at the bar. Like all the other bars and clubs in Newport, once the band played, seating would be at a premium as the entire room transformed into a dance floor. Movement would be limited to a shake and shimmy as people crammed the space. Kelly and Maddie continually scanned the crowd as they sipped their chardonnays and leaned into one another's ear to be heard over the boisterous music.

"Oh my, look at this clown!" Kelly exclaimed.

Maddie turned her head to see a man gyrating his way through the crowd toward them. His slick hair, partially unbuttoned shirt, and thick gold chain around his neck caused him to stand out against the typically preppy guys that frequented the Newport scene.

"Good evening, ladies, how you all doin' tonight?"

Maddie tried to be polite but Kelly openly laughed at his line.

"Could I perhaps buy you lovely girls a drink?"

Kelly rolled her eyes. "Seriously?"

"No thanks," said Maddie "I'm all set for now."

But Bob Lackey wasn't going anywhere. He called out to the bartender in a husky baritone voice. "Scuse me, can I get another beer here?" Which sounded like, "Can I get anoth-ah bee-ah he-ah."

Bob's pursuit of Maddie was tenacious. She had to admit he was a pretty good-looking guy, even if his corporal expressiveness and fashion style bordered on the comical. There was something about the intensity of his stare mixed with his humor that made for an alluring combination.

A couple drinks later, Maddie's wall of doubt had crumbled. Despite the warning faces Kelly had made, Maddie gave Bob her phone number.

# TWENTY-TWO

Watching Sally's young supple ass shake as he thrust into her, James Cooper felt compelled to give it a sharp strike with the full palm of his hand. Her pillow muffled yelp was exactly what he needed to hear. He leaned forward grabbed her hair, flipped her over and drove his member into her mouth.

"Harder, harder," he demanded followed by a deep groan as he released into her throat.

Initially, his encounters with Sally had helped to satisfy his desires. She was enjoyable and very convenient, but lately, he felt himself wanting something even more... forbidden.

# TWENTY-THREE

Bob would not be slipping in shit today. He had made a date. Not just with some broad but with a fine young lady, Maddie Marcelle.

Mr. D's guard opened the door to the office.

"You got the money?" Cosimo barked from behind a heavy, dark mahogany desk.

Bob was already vehemently nodding his head. "Yes sir, I do."

"Sit down. I gotta take this call," ordered Cosimo.

Cosimo picked up one of three cell phones on his desk. "Just the man I was waiting to hear from. Everything set-up? Good, well I don't have to go all the way to the islands for hot weather. Yeah, hot as balls up here. I'll see you when you get back."

Cosimo was now visibly happier than when Bob had first walked in. "Mikey, make Bob and me a cappuccino, actually make mine iced. You want iced?" Cosimo pointed at Bob.

"Sure, iced is good." Bob could almost hear the jingling as he landed in gold.

# TWENTY-FOUR

"**P**erfect beach day," Winston commented as he held open the passenger door of a polished, black Range Rover for Maddie to climb in.

She pushed her canvas bag onto the floor and asked, "Do I need to grab a beach chair?"

Winston grinned. "Not for where we're going," he said and closed her door. Winston executed a three-point turn and headed back down the tree-lined driveway.

Maddie expectantly stared at Winston's chiseled profile. Nothing. "So are we going on a mystery ride?"

Winston glanced over. "No, we're going to Bailey's Beach Club."

*Okay, the mystery part is still intact,* she thought. Maddie knew Bailey's was an exclusive private beach club, where money alone did not bestow membership. Gaining access was about legacy and pedigree. For years rumors had circulated about a famous New York real estate mogul, with later shocking political success, who had been denied entrance to the beach club despite all his wealth. Gauche, new money held no sway over the membership committee at Bailey's. "I'll admit I'm curious about what goes on behind that grey and yellow façade that makes the club so elite."

"It's not what happens there so much as it is who is there to make it happen."

Maddie's eyes squinted. "Thanks, Winston, that clears it up," she commented sarcastically.

Winston reached over and squeezed Maddie's hand.

~~~~~~~~~

Winston circled around Maddie like a shark, then popped up next to her. Tiny beads of water shimmered and glistened on his smooth, toned runner's body. His body slid around hers, but much too briefly in her mind, as they splashed and bobbed in the surf. Laughing, Maddie turned to grab Winston when she was suddenly hit in the face by a wave. Water flooded her nose and mouth. She was coughing to stop the burn of salt and expel the water. She felt herself rising up and was afraid she was being carried out by a wave, but as her head cleared she realized it was Winston's strong arms around her, lifting her up into his chest.

"Don't worry. I've got you. I think it's time for us to take a break."

Her feet sank into the wet sand helping to anchor her as Winston set her down at the edge of the water and led her to their beach chairs. Maddie crossed her arms over her shoulders to warm herself. The sensation of choking had left her chilled.

"You look cold. I'll go get us some towels." Winston offered.

Maddie watched him walk away. She wondered if Winston would ever open up and try to be more than a concerned friend. *Maybe he just doesn't want to show a public display of affection at the club, or maybe his impeccable manners are preventing him from just letting go. He's definitely holding back. I mean, he hasn't even kissed me yet! He's probably just concerned about me wanting to take things slow, and the fact that I told him I want to keep my options open. What if I went too far telling him about Jared? What if we're stuck in the friend zone?* Maddie closed her eyes. She could feel her friend Kelly pop up on her shoulder to tell her *'stop over analyzing, stop jumping to conclusions, just relax and be in the moment!'*

Winston picked up two fluffy yellow and white, striped beach towels from a basket in his private cabana. *This has gone on too long. I have to do what it takes to show Madison I'm serious. And if Jared keeps sniffing around, I'll do what it takes to show him I'm serious.*

Maddie opened her eyes and saw Winston was heading back toward her. She felt the butterflies flicker to life again in her stomach. She was very attracted to him and definitely living in the moment now.

"Here we go." Winston wrapped a towel around her. He kept one arm secured around her shoulder. His other hand came up and gently brushed her jawbone then his hand slid under the back of her hair.

Maddie was aware that her heart was pounding so fast it was nearly audible. *Surely he can hear it?*

Winston looked into her eyes, bent his head and softly pushed his lips onto her wanting mouth. His lips slowly retreated then pushed again. Maddie felt electricity jolt through every nerve in her body. It was ninety-three degrees out but she gave an involuntary shiver. He pressed his chest against hers and held her tighter. His nose nuzzled her

71

ear, he ran his tongue along her earlobe then whispered, "There, are you warm now?"

She couldn't speak. The air in her lungs seemed to be missing. He had taken her breath away. All she could do was simply nod in agreement.

# TWENTY-FIVE

Jared stepped into his office to find Ken sitting behind Jared's desk tapping on his computer. "Welcome back. I see you've made yourself at home with my things again. How was your trip?"

Ken didn't bother to look up but answered, "Trip was fine."

Jared sat himself on the edge of his desk. "You never told me where you were going."

This time Ken glanced at Jared. "I was out of the country on some family business."

"So how are your parents?" Jared inquired.

Ken's eyes remained on Jared's computer as he busily typed. "Fine."

"Is your mom still running the mahjong league of Florence?"

"Probably, I didn't see them on this trip, it was just business."

Jared leaned forward to look around at the computer screen. "What on earth are you doing on my computer that it is so important?"

"Bigger question Jared, is why do you have a note for a helicopter today on your schedule?"

Jared stood up and walked around behind Ken, who had pulled up Jared's daily calendar. "I thought you were going over the books, Ken."

The Sunday before Ken had left for his trip Jared had called Ken intending to reveal that he had external auditors looking at the books, and they had found some red flags. But he decided at the last second to wait and see if the auditors had any real information to give him before worrying Ken.

"Yeah, I took care of everything before I left. Everything is in order, we're making money, no worries. Now tell me about the helicopter?" Ken spun the leather desk chair around to face Jared.

"Not that it's any of your business—"

"Your business has always been my business," Ken interrupted.

"I rented a helicopter for this afternoon to take out a lovely young lady named Maddie Marcelle."

Ken's brow furrowed in confusion. "Why? Does she have something to do with the computer business?"

"No. You know I keep my professional life separate from my personal life. I don't like to mix business with pleasure. Maddie has her own money, she's really down to earth, and you know better than anyone I have not had a connection with a girl for quite a while!"

Ken bristled at the idea of Jared out with this girl. He thought of telling Jared he seriously doubted some insipid little debutant could ever give him what he needs – but he didn't want to piss Jared off.

"Yes sir, enjoy your day," was all Ken said before Jared left for his date with Maddie.

# TWENTY-SIX

**M**addie paced a loop between her kitchen and the mudroom pausing to peer out the window in the door that faced the driveway. *Jared should be here at any minute. Should I tell him at the beginning of the date, or wait for it to come up in conversation? I don't want him to think I'm not interested, but I don't want him to think we're exclusive, and I really don't want him to think I'm a whore.* Maddie's nervous energy had her picking at her fingernails as she crossed into the mudroom again, this time she saw a large SUV roaring up the driveway like a black stallion.

Maddie pointed at Jared's shoes as he stepped into the mudroom. "No shoes, please."

Jared laughed. "Seriously?"

Maddie couldn't help thinking back to the apartment she had shared with Joe. He was always stomping around in his work boots, leaving a trail of grime she was expected to clean up.

"Yeah, I got a thing about shoes in the house, it grosses me out."

Jared slid his leather loafers off. "I can respect that" and paced through the mudroom into the sunlit, open kitchen. He surveyed the cottage. "This is really nice; great view with a cozy, happy vibe. My house feels so austere. Maybe I need a woman's touch?" Jared turned back to face Maddie.

Her lips were pursed and it seemed as if she had been holding her breath as she suddenly blurted out, "Listen, before we do anything, I need to tell you something. I know this is our first date and I don't want to set a negative tone but I need you to know that I'm still seeing Winston and he knows I am interested in dating you too." She paused to take in a needed breath. Before Jared could respond she continued. "I need you to understand, about year and a half ago I was engaged to be married. I caught my fiancé being unfaithful. I was so devastated that I haven't felt comfortable talking to a guy, let alone dating a guy, until now. And now I really want to just date. No expectations, just get to know each other. It's a lot to ask but would you be willing to date me knowing I'm seeing someone else too?" Her hope-filled eyes were open wide. Her thumb was anxiously pushing under her short nails.

Jared's face became void of emotion as he responded to her. "So what if I'm also seeing another person?"

Maddie looked stunned as she slowly asked, "Are you?"

His playful smile returned. "No. Look, Maddie, I felt a connection with you. I like you. I want to get to know you better, even if it means sharing you-- for now. So are you ready for our date?"

Maddie was visibly relieved and gave him an enthusiastic nod. "Yes!"

As Jared settled Maddie into his car he checked, "So, I hope you're not afraid of heights?"

Maddie narrowed her eyes and gave him a puzzled look. "I'm not."

Jared began driving. "And I hope you're feeling adventurous?"

"How adventurous?"

"I got us a helicopter. You told me you like history and I thought we could take in Newport's past and present from the air."

"As long as I don't have to jump out of the helicopter, it sounds fun."

~~~~~~~~

Maddie had been on some impressive dates with Winston but zooming around with a bird's eye view of Aquidneck Island gave the term whirlwind romance a new meaning.

Maddie sank back into the passenger seat as Jared's SUV wound its way up a shrub-lined driveway. At the top an imposing Victorian house, its shingles weathered deep brown, loomed over Jamestown harbor.

"Welcome to my home," Jared announced.

Maddie took in the dark, brooding atmosphere of the house as Jared gave her a tour. She noted that each hollow space he occupied seemed to brighten as he passed through.

Out on the shady covered porch they watched sailboats gracefully glide back and forth across the channel between Newport and Jamestown. An apron-clad caterer served them baby lettuce topped with sweet, meaty lobster salad.

"What do you know about wine?" Jared asked as he tipped a deep pour of white wine into Maddie's glass.

"I know I prefer white to red. Beyond that I'm clueless."

"Well, we have plenty of this sauvignon blanc. It's from the Marlborough region of New Zealand. Let me know what you think."

Maddie sipped. "Crisp, citrusy like grapefruit."

"For someone who thinks she's clueless, you have a great palate," Jared remarked.

"That's good to know; for years I was with a beer drinker and that's all we ever had."

"Beer drinker, huh?"

Maddie quickly changed the subject. "Tell me how you know about wine?" She refused to allow any more thoughts of Joe to creep onto this fabulous date. She listened in earnest curiosity as Jared wove together tales of his first encounters with 'good wine' in Tuscany with his friend Ken.

Several hours later the magic of sunset colored Jared's light brown, wavy hair. *The perfect end to a perfect date*, Maddie thought as they finally made their way off the porch and down to Jared's vehicle. The drive over the long arching Pell Bridge, which connects Jamestown to Newport, was filled with quiet banter and laughter. Maddie didn't need Kelly's voice in her head to remind her to focus on the moment. Jared had her complete attention.

~~~~~~~~~

As they approached the door to her house Maddie groped around inside her purse. "If I could find my keys we could get in and I could make you some coffee."

Jared reached out and gently snagged her arm. "Listen, Maddie, I want to respect that you're not ready to jump into a relationship yet. So, I'll be a gentleman and say good night here."

Maddie looked up, a bit surprised he was ready to end the evening here but as his face came closer to hers, her worries fell away. His lips softly grazed hers then pressed into a lingering kiss. The warm tiny needles that started a quiver below her dress quickly spread up to the nerves on the edge of her mouth. As Jared allowed his lips to slowly retreat she dug her fingers into his shirt and used it to pull him back into her. She wanted to feel more of his body entwined on hers but regained her composure. Gently she pulled away from him and took a step back.

"Whew," Jared blew out a long audible sigh. "I think I might need to go home and take a cold shower." He scooped up Maddie's hands, pressed them to his mouth, and quietly stated, "I really enjoyed your company. I would love to see you again. So, please don't commit all your time to Winston. Okay?"

Maddie reached up and brushed a lock of hair from his forehead, "Okay. I enjoyed your company too. Give me a call. I would love to go out again."

# TWENTY-SEVEN

Bzz bzz bzz-- He opened one eye and shifted his head from the pillow to see which phone was ringing. It was the secret line; which could only mean one thing, a late-night rendezvous. He grabbed the phone, rolled onto his back, and answered, "So I thought you were a gentleman?"

"I am," was the response.

"Well, gentlemen are supposed to be in bed at this hour."

"I plan to be in bed, just not mine. I'll be in at your place in ten minutes."

"Yes, sir." He smirked as he clicked off the call and thought, *proof I have him where I want him.*

~~~~~~~~

Two hours later, he pulled the other man back down onto the bed. "Wait, it's so late. Just spend the night here."

"You know that can't happen," the other man said.

He brushed his hand through the other man's hair. "Come on," he whispered, "just once."

The other man slapped his hand away. "Stop pushing this!" the other man shouted as he got up and stood beside the bed.

He was left on the bed and clearly agitated. "Oh right, because you have to go running back to her," he spewed.

"You leave her out of this. She has nothing to do with us."

"Well, I guess if it's not her it's everything else you have going on. You know someday your big, secret affair with me is going to come out and then what will you do?!"

Instantly the other man swooped down grabbed his jaw and forcefully pressed his fingers into the bone. "You had better damn well hope that what goes on between us and the rest of my life never, ever, meet up. Understand?"

Through gritted teeth, he answered, "Yes, sir."

The other man stood upright again. "Good. Now stop talking and put your mouth to good use."

The blonde man on the bed rose up onto his elbows, "Yes, sir."

# TWENTY-EIGHT

"Come in." Maddie grabbed Kelly's hand and pulled her into her home. It had been another restless night of sleep. Maddie was grateful for the distraction Kelly provided from her tiredness.

"So, I brought some invitation samples. You have such good taste. I need you to help me decide."

Kelly spread a smattering of cardstock and books onto Maddie's kitchen island.

"Well, I don't know about good taste, I just know what I like." *At least I used to. Now I talk to myself inside my head before I make decisions,* Maddie thought.

Kelly glanced around Maddie's home. "Look at this place, it's gorgeous. God knows you could afford to have an interior decorator but you did all this yourself. Good taste."

Maddie shook her head as she took in her eclectic mix of casual furniture dotted with antique tables and chests. Though some items were quite expensive; she had not sought them out for their value, but rather chose them because she liked the look of a traditional design and appreciated good craftsmanship. This stylish, elegant, yet comfortable oasis she had created truly suited her personality. *Well, I must still have some sense, I love the home I made here.* "Let's just see what you brought and we'll try to narrow it down."

"What do you think of this?" Kelly held up a heart-shaped ivory card with red swirly letters.

Maddie crinkled her mouth. "If you like it, then it's nice."

"I asked if YOU like it. I want your opinion. Come on, help me out. Maddie? Maddie?"

Maddie was running her index finger over the raised letters spelling Mr. & Mrs. Her thoughts twirled around the idea of Mrs. *Right now I would be Mrs. Joseph Vento. Mrs. Stop Talking, Mrs. You Don't Know Nothin', Mrs. Get Me Another Beer, Mrs. Cheated On and Lied To...*

Kelly waved a card in front of Maddie's eyes. "Hey, where did you just go? Is it Joe?"

Maddie couldn't speak. She should be over this by now. Over her anger. Over her fear that Joe might show up and hurt her again.

"Maddie, I'm here for you. Is it Winston?"

*Focus. The only way to get over something is to just go through it! Winston? Yes, let's talk about Winston.* "Sorry, yes, it's Winston. I was just thinking about how different Jared and Winston are from each other, but I love spending time with both of them. I mean when I am with one, I'm not thinking about the other. But, I'm a little worried I might get in too deep with one of them, and I don't know what I would do if they wanted to date other girls too." Maddie flicked the card in her hand onto the island. She let out an exasperated sigh. "This is all just so new to me."

Kelly gave a reassuring smile. "Hey, it's okay. You're single, they're single, and no one is in too deep. You're just having fun, right? Are they dating anyone else?"

"Winston told me within the crowd he circulates, marriages are basically arranged. So he's acted the part of the playboy to avoid it. He also told me I'm the first girl he's dated seriously and he wants to keep it that way."

Kelly grimaced. "Okay. Sounds deep on his part. What about Jared?"

Maddie walked over to her refrigerator. "You want some wine?"

"It's one o'clock in the afternoon!" Kelly mock protested.

"Great! That means it's seven p.m. in Italy, which is where this wine is from so it is begging to be popped open. Since you asked about Jared, he has broadened my wine horizon so I am going to extend yours too."

Kelly made a show of swirling and sniffing her wine. "Pinot Gris. Well, it tastes different than Chardonnay." Kelly took another sip. "I think I like it."

Maddie nodded. "Tastes like a good summer wine. Refreshing, right?"

"Agreed. Back to Jared now," Kelly prompted.

"Jared is more of a mystery than Winston. I know he is interested in me, but he works odd hours so we talk or text at random times. Not like the daily morning check-in routine I have with Winston. He outright told me he is not seeing anyone else, so I know any concern I have is just in my head."

"Okay. So let it go and enjoy!" Kelly pushed her wine glass forward for a refill.

"If only it was that easy," Maddie muttered.

Kelly narrowed her eyes. "Why would it not be?"

*Oh, I do not want a conversation about my crazy nerves. Deflect. Either way, she'll have something to say. At least this will be productive.* "Well, now there's Bob." Maddie prepared for the attack.

Kelly opened her mouth and launched the first strike. "Bob? The idiot from the bar Bob? What about Bob?!"

"He just seems so fun. I agreed to go out on a date with him."

"Everyone seems fun when you're drinking in a bar, Maddie. He's slick and slimy! The kind of guy Jack would arrest. You should not-"

"Stop!" Maddie did not want to fight with Kelly. "I am going on one date. As you keep reminding me, I am single and I should only be having fun. I have no interest in a serious relationship, right now." Maddie slid onto a chair next to Kelly and softened her tone. "I do listen to you. I do appreciate your advice, but I am going to go out with Bob. Now, speaking of Jack, how is the new job going?"

Kelly pushed around some sample invitations then took a big gulp of wine. Her expression of resignation let Maddie know she was ready to change the subject. "Jack is really getting into being a detective. He respects the hell out of his Captain. He's been on a learning curve, which he likes because he says it's a good challenge, and his hours now line up with my hours at the hospital so we get to see each other all the time."

Maddie reached out and squeezed Kelly's hand. "You are my best friend and you know how I feel about Jack. You are marrying each other and I am over the moon happy for you both. The fact that your careers line up is like the stars lining up. This is meant to be."

"Thank you." Kelly reciprocated the squeeze then softly asked, "Do Jared and Winston know about Bob?"

"I am dating out in the open here, Kelly. No secrets. I want everyone to know where they stand, so I don't hurt anyone."

"I know you're talking about Joe, Maddie. You are not Joe. I know you doubt it sometimes, but you are your own person. You are honest and you are doing all the right things to move on. "

*I guess actions speak louder than crazy thoughts. I am putting myself out there. I'm trying to move on,* Maddie thought. "I'm trying Kelly. It's all I can do." She felt like someone she remembered, someone with an opinion. "By the way I don't like that heart-shaped invitation. It's too cliché."

# TWENTY NINE

His voice came from behind her. "You're a stupid, silly girl. You think everyone is so nice, so helpful." She could feel his solid body, so close, talking in her ear. "It's probably not your fault that you are so naïve, it's the way people have always treated you, like a beautiful flower growing along the side of a busy sidewalk. Everyone steps over it, or around it, never trampling it as they would the ugly bare concrete or even mashed down grass next to you. You trusted my intentions but maybe you should have trusted your own instincts." Strong hands were holding her down.

She couldn't see his face. She could never see his face. She felt trapped. She desperately needed to know, "Who are you?"

"You know me. This will teach you."

Maddie's eyes bolted awake. Her chest heaving, she sat up. It was dark. The only light in the living room came from the moon through the windows. She fumbled around on the coffee table for her phone to call Kelly, then stopped. *What time is it? Kelly's probably snuggled up in bed with Jack. I can't go cry to her because I had another bad dream. It feels so real. Is it just a dream?* A sense of deep foreboding filled her mind. She wanted to fight it. *I am not a silly little girl. I am in control.*

"I am in control!" she shouted in the empty room.

# THIRTY

Bob swayed down the dock next to his condominium along Newport harbor. In the winter he lived in the condo, but his only source of legitimate income came from renting the place out in the summer and residing on his power boat at the dock. On a boat, every inch of space is useful and usable and a boat of thirty feet is livable, for a bachelor. Bob finished tidying the boat up and checked his watch. Maddie was due there in about five minutes.

She showed up looking like she had just fallen out of a sailing catalog. Bob reached out to help her aboard. She gave a small squeal as she bridged the gap between the dock and the deck of the boat.

"Never been on a boat before?' Bob inquired.

"How could you tell?" Maddie stylishly posed and showed off her new Sperry topsiders, white capri pants, topped with a navy and white striped shirt.

"Boating looks good on you!" Bob declared. "Come on I'll show you where you can stow your bag."

Maddie put her things on a berth cushion below deck and headed back up the stairs of the companionway. Bob was sitting on a long, tufted Captain's bench.

"Don't worry." Bob patted the space next to him and motioned for her to join him behind the wheel. "Nothing to it. Just like a car on the water, but with fewer rules and you can drink!" Bob fired up the engine, then tottered along the starboard side to cast off.

Bob glanced over at Maddie as they sputtered out of the inner harbor and headed out towards Beavertail point at the end of Jamestown, *time to impress*, he thought. He jammed the throttle forward. As the engine accelerated so did the noise, which made conversation difficult but the ride exciting. The boat leaped up, floated on the air for a second or two then crashed down onto the water only to repeat the cycle in another instant. The wind thrashed Maddie's hair but she couldn't pull it into a ponytail as she didn't dare let go of her grip on the bottom of the seat for fear of tumbling off it.

"Are you okay?" Bob hollered into her ear.

"Whoohoo!" she shouted. The air whipping around her gave her a chill and she cuddled up to the side of Bob's body. Having slammed around Narragansett Bay for about an hour Bob turned the vessel back toward Newport harbor. The return trip was much calmer, and warmer, as Bob eased the throttle back to a slow cruise. He kept a cooler on deck next to the steering helm and made sure that Maddie's plastic cup was filled with cheap white wine. Although she had tried to sip her wine slowly on the ride back, the combination of warm weather and sun reflecting off the water had encouraged her to drink more than she should have.

When they arrived back at his dock slip Bob could see Maddie was feeling a little tipsy. He was on her like a monkey on a cupcake. Unlike Winston and Jared, Bob was an aggressive kisser. Bob's advances were not unwelcome but a few bottles of water were a bit more welcome at this point. She extricated herself from Bob's octopus grope and retrieved a water bottle from the galley fridge. She quickly polished off one bottle and reached in for another. Settling herself on the opposite side of the main salon, she looked across the table at Bob and steered the conversation towards food.

"I don't think I've eaten today, except for a hardboiled egg this morning. Are you hungry?"

Bob was hungry but what he wanted didn't require a trip off the boat.

Maddie saw the glint in his eye. *Oh crap. I don't think I can handle round two of his tongue.* "It's pretty stuffy down here and we've been sitting all day. I think I'll just grab my bag and go for a walk around town."

Bob was unprepared for this turn of event. *What the hell's going on? Girls usually have their tops off by now and I've at least banged them before we go looking for food. She is pretty hot though, whatever.* "You're right. A walk would be good. Maybe we'll grab dinner too?"

Bob helped Maddie hop down onto the dock, "Wait right here, I gotta get my keys to lock this hatch."

He disappeared below, opened a drawer in the galley, looked down at his wallet and keys and reached in.

~~~~~~~~~

All along Thames Street clumps of people slowly plodded along the sidewalk as they pushed into and spilled out of the shops, cafes, and restaurants. Maddie and Bob were sometimes forced onto the street as they tried to pass the herds and make their way to a place to eat. Bob turned towards the sound of a band playing Jimmy Buffet music at the end of Waite's Wharf. He directed Maddie in front of him so he could watch her backside and the roving packs of young girls wandering along the wharf.

The outdoor bar was already full and the tables lining the edge of the dock were filling up too.

"Looks like we got here just in time," Maddie commented.

Bob's words were directed toward Maddie, but his head was turned away toward the bar. "Yeah, always busy here in the summer. Hey, Dave guess you didn't die last night! Ha, ha!" He turned to face Maddie. "Buddy of mine, always here. I like to bust his balls. Ya know?"

"Yes, I see that. Let's grab that table over there." Maddie wanted to be as far away from the bar filled with men who were eyeing her like a lamb who had just wandered into the wolves' den.

*Oh, well. Party at the bar will have to wait for another night,* Bob thought. *I know the look of a woman in need of some one on one time with me.* He took Maddie by the hand and led her to a table. Bob ordered a beer and a house chardonnay for Maddie.

*Red flag;* for an instant it was just like being out with Joe as the thought crossed through her mind she called out to the server. "Actually, I'll have a seltzer water with lemon, please." *Score for me. He's not Joe and I can handle myself.*

Bob wasn't used to being contradicted by a woman. *This one's feisty, probably a lawyer.* "What do you do for a living, Maddie?"

"I used to be a nurse." She paused, not sure how much she wanted to share about herself yet. His deep blue eyes drew her in, dancing closer to get to know her then retreating to hide their own secrets. She offered up a bit more information. "I got burned out of the hospital scene. I would get too attached to people and if I couldn't help them, I became depressed. Then I was a private nurse to one of the best men I have ever known, but he passed on."

The server carefully set a large cup of beer down in front of Bob just as the foam slid over the edge, along with a bowl of popcorn. Maddie squirted a lemon wedge into her water and they tapped their plastic cups together,

"Cheers!" they exclaimed simultaneously.

"So what do you do now?" Bob asked.

"Well, I'm trying to figure that out, but I'm pretty lucky because I have time to do just that." Maddie didn't feel comfortable revealing her situation. Experience had taught her that most people loved to talk about themselves. Her stomach rumbled with hunger. She quickly changed the subject, happy to dive into the popcorn bowl. "So, what about you Bob, what's your story?"

Bob sat back, crunching his popcorn, "I'm in business for myself."

Maddie figured there had to be more and waited for him to finish probing around his mouth for stuck bits of kernels. He seemed satisfied that he had extracted all he could from his mouthful of popcorn but had moved on to a new subject. He was filling her in on the joys of blasting out to Block Island on his boat and the outrageous party scene there.

Bob finished guzzling down a post-dinner beer. He was feeling confident that his stories had impressed her and she would be ready to loosen up back on his boat. He signaled for the check.

Their server brushed by the table and set the bill down in a small black leather folio. Bob feigned a pat down of his pockets. "Damn it!" he exclaimed.

Maddie looked concerned. "What's wrong?"

"I forgot my wallet on the boat."

"No worries Bob. I can pay for it."

"No, this is embarrassing. I'll just go run back to the boat and get it."

But Maddie insisted. "Don't worry, it's no problem at all." She heaved her stylish leather bag onto her lap.

"Nice bag," Bob commented.

"Thanks. One of my inheritance splurges."

"Inheritance?" Bob sounded surprised and tried not to sound overly excited.

"I don't really like to talk much about it, but it's why I have the time to figure out what's next for me."

"Well, I hope what's next is another date with me so I can pay you back for dinner." Bob leaned close. "Or maybe we could work something out back on my boat?"

~~~~~~~~

Maddie replayed her date with Bob as she drove home. Processing information aloud had become a habit for her. "The guy is over the top. He's like a cartoon character; overbuilt, over opinionated, loud... sort of funny."

Dinner conversation had revealed little about Bob, except that he had a crass, quick wit and clearly thought his escapades were impressive.

"He is a good-looking guy. But I can't believe he actually thought I would go back to his boat with him tonight. And I still don't know what he does for work. Although, who am I to judge. People probably wonder the same about me."

Her mind looped through the boat ride and dinner once more. "Well, I don't see this going too far. He is entertaining. I'd probably go on another date."

~~~~~~~~~

It didn't matter he could not entice Maddie back to his boat after dinner because there would be another opportunity on the next date. *Her shell might be a bit harder to crack than most, but I can do it,* Bob thought.

Bob was headed to one of the massage parlors off Broadway to relieve himself. A loophole in Rhode Island law made prostitution legal, so long as it occurred indoors.

*She passed the wallet test with flying colors. And there's an inheritance! Hell, she might even be a good cook. She's not just a winner. She's the jackpot and what a hot looking smoke show. That's the girl that stays in your brain and leaves you jumping at the chance to see her again. The best part is she seems to have no idea she has that effect on people. Seems classy. She may need a little more effort, but I can work her over,* Bob thought.

# THIRTY-ONE

Winston let himself into the mudroom of Maddie's home, slipped off his Topsiders, and called out for her.

She walked around the corner to find Winston sitting cross-legged on a bench next to the door. "Hi." She looked at his bare feet. "I see you remembered the rules."

"You realize I don't usually follow rules, Madison, but you seem so serious. So, I will try for you."

Maddie stuffed a sweatshirt into a canvas bag. "That's good. My ex-fiancé didn't seem to care about rules either at least not when it came to our relationship."

"Madison, is something bothering you?"

"No. Well, yes." Maddie paused she could feel all the words, bolstered by emotion, rising up fast and hard in her throat. She couldn't hold back and allowed them to tumble out. "It's just that I really like spending time with you. I want to keep things moving along but I know I shouldn't be in one serious relationship. So, I'm also seeing Jared. You met him at the New York Yacht Club." She watched Winston's eyes grow wide but she couldn't stop now. Before he could speak, she continued her effusive confessional. "And there's another guy. Bob. I think I might want to date him too but I feel guilty when I'm with you.

I feel like I'm cheating somehow and after my ex-fiancé cheated on me, it was devastating! I would never want you, or anyone, to feel the way I did. And I'm worried that you might want to start seeing other women too. I know it's hypocritical but I don't think I would like that very much." She took in a much-needed breath. Her left thumb was steadily grinding under the fingernails of her right hand as she anxiously awaited Winston's response.

"Okay. I guess a lot is bothering you." Winston guided her to sit down next to him on the bench. "First, we have talked about this and I assure you there is no other woman I want to date or be with. Next, I get that you are not me and you need some time to figure things out. When you get this dating thing out of your system I will be right here, where I have always been, ready for the next level of our relationship."

Maddie shifted herself onto Winston's lap and sank into a deep kiss.

~~~~~~~~~

The southwest breeze was coming up. Maddie raked her fingers through her hair and drew it back into a ponytail. She tottered down the New York Yacht Club's floating dock behind Winston until they reached the end. Winston motioned his hand like Vanna White revealing a puzzle letter.

"Now this is what I imagined a classic sailboat to look like. It's so pretty." Maddie gushed.

"She is so pretty," Winston corrected. "All boats are female. And of course, she is. She's a Morris." Winston confidently grinned as if Maddie understood this premier yacht was at the high-end of cruising boats.

"I don't know what that means. I've actually never been on a sailboat," she confessed.

"Have you ever been on any boat before?" Winston asked.

"Once. It was really loud."

"Powerboat, yes?"

Maddie nodded an affirmative.

"Then I have a lot to teach you. Let's start with these lines." Winston handed her a coil of red and white striped rope.

As Winston hauled up the boat's sails he gave Maddie a running commentary of what he was doing and why. "So the line in this jam cleat loosens the vang."

She did not understand a word of the seemingly foreign language he was speaking.

~~~~~~~

Their boat nosed away from the dock and headed out of the harbor toward Castle Hill. Winston was at the helm explaining how sailing the boat directly into the wind would essentially stop the boat and they would be 'in irons'.

"We're getting awfully close to those rocks," Maddie nervously called out.

"Correct. Because we are about to tack around. You see we are zigzagging across the wind." Winston directed her to a winch with a rope spiraled around it. "When I tell you, you are going to release that line the way I showed you back at the dock. Understand?"

Maddie nodded her head. Her heart pounded with anticipation.

Winston called out, "Ready about." He turned the boat's massive wheel. Then commanded, "Hard alee. Now, Madison. Let the line completely off the winch."

She did as she was instructed.

"Good. Now hurry, move to the other side of the cockpit."

At the same instant, Winston pitched to the opposite side of the boat, yanked another red and white line, quickly coiled it around the opposing winch, and pulled the slack tight. The forward sail had swung around to the other side of the boat. Suddenly the yacht heaved. The length of its hull upended from the water.

Maddie frantically screamed, "Help! We're going over!" She desperately clung to the cockpit's cushions, trying not to slide overboard as the boat continued to tilt. Panic consumed her as she watched Winston double over. When he raised his head, he was still laughing. "What is going on?" she yelled. She crawled against gravity to get over to him and smacked him squarely on his shoulder.

"I'm sorry Madison. I've never seen someone react so passionately when we heel over." He continued to chuckle. "Don't worry we are not going to capsize. We'll only have to tack like that again a few more times. Once we round the point we will be on a broad reach and we can relax for a while."

She nodded her head. The only words she understood from his explanation were 'relax a while.'

By the time they had completed their last tack past Castle Hill Maddie's confidence to predict the action required to sail upwind had grown.

"Okay, smooth sailing now," Winston announced as they rounded out of the bay and cruised past Brenton State Park. "Here, come take the wheel."

Apprehensively, Maddie slid in front of Winston at the helm. He pressed from behind her, guiding her hands to take positions at ten o'clock and two o'clock on the wheel. She felt the wind slap her face as the waves rushed along the length of the boat. Winston bent his head to speak in her ear.

"There," he pointed toward the bow, "see those little ripples, where the water is darker?"

She scanned ahead then exclaimed, "Yes, up there!"

"That's a puff of wind. Let's turn the wheel toward it."

As Maddie made the steering adjustment, she said, "This is hard!"

Winston laughed. "This is sailing. It requires skill. If it was easy, you would be on a power boat!"

Maddie was exhilarated. She worked to control the boat as the sails harnessed the wind propelling the yacht through the waves.

Winston gestured to the port side. "See that house over there?"

Maddie looked over to the stony shoreline carved with rocky coves. An imposing stone mansion dominated a jagged peninsula.

"How could I not see that house? It's enormous!"

"It is a lot of house. Thank goodness we have a staff to take care of it. Although they'll be departing soon to accompany my parents to our house in France. Leaving me to rattle around by myself."

Maddie craned her head over her shoulder to face Winston. "That's your home? It seems daunting."

"Well, it's my family home. Has been for generations. It's called Seafair. I live there with my parents."

"What about that little house, tucked inside the cove?"

"That point of land and all the buildings are ours. The house inside the cove with the dock is our boathouse. Now, trying to navigate in there without experience is daunting!"

~~~~~~~~~~

More was expressed in the comfort of quiet than could have been said in words on the downwind leg back to the New York Yacht Club. The shared experience combined with the strikingly beautiful surroundings cemented the easiness between Winston and Maddie. But deep in the recess of her mind, she wondered how she could continue to date more than one man.

# THIRTY-TWO

"Thank goodness, I thought you forgot!" Kelly exclaimed.

Maddie gave Kelly a hug. "I'm your maid of honor you can always count on me." She looked around the small floral shop. Every space, high and low, was packed with greenery, flowers, vases, and ribbon.

A slightly plump lady with wavy, white hair directed Maddie and Kelly up an iron spiral staircase in the back corner of the shop. In the center of the floral loft was a round table with four basket weave backed chairs. The table displayed photo albums and a stack of sticky-note pads and a few pens.

"I pulled out some albums featuring the colors we discussed Miss Hurley. I'll let you ladies look through to get some ideas. I'll come back up in a few minutes and we can make some decisions," said the friendly shop owner.

Maddie and Kelly watched her waddle back down the curved stairs before they started chatting.

"Jack got the promotion! Which means I can get bigger arrangements," Kelly shared in a hushed voice with a big smile.

Maddie returned the smile and offered, "Kelly let me pay for the wedding flowers. You can get whatever you want."

Kelly suddenly looked solemn. "Maddie I really need you to listen to me on this. Having money has not changed you and that's a good thing. But if you start paying for me then things will change between us. Eventually, you will become resentful and I will become expectant."

"So, you want me to pretend I don't have an inheritance?"

"Not at all. Let's just keep things the way they have always been. We each pay our own way. We can do nice things for each other, take each other out for drinks, but stay true to ourselves. Nothing too ostentatious."

"I can do that. I don't want to be someone who's out of touch with reality. I had a great meeting with my lawyer, Mr. Shorey last week. We did some estate planning and more importantly set up some charitable plans. Which makes me feel better about the few nice treats I've purchased for myself." Maddie clenched her teeth and shrugged sheepishly at Kelly.

Kelly gave her the affirmation she needed to hear. "But nothing over the top. You bought a small house on a beautiful piece of real estate, a nice car but not something totally impractical, some clothing and..." Kelly's eyes trailed down to Maddie's purse.

Maddie filled in Kelly's sentence, "And a handbag that's over the top. Unless you think of it as an investment bag!"

"Yeah, the bag is a bit much. You might want to keep that 'investment bag' habit in check."

They both laughed at the absurdity of a handbag being an investment piece.

"So, I should cancel my order for the pet white tiger?" Maddie snickered.

Kelly smiled. "Just pass me that photo book."

A round face popped up over the top stair at the landing. "Sounds like you ladies are having a good time. Have you made any decisions yet?"

Maddie looked from the shop owner to Kelly. "About life, yes. About flowers, no."

# THIRTY-THREE

Bob was settled in his usual corner booth at the back of Gordon's Greasy Spoon on lower Thames Street in Newport. Brenda didn't need to take his order; his eggs had been cracked on the griddle about five seconds after he walked in. She automatically filled the coffee cup in front of the black and white paper tower rising in front of Bob's face. A top corner of the tower collapsed and Bob peered out. "Good Morning, Brenda. Gonna be a hot one today."

"Sure is, Bob. Maybe I'll head to the beach when I get outta here at noon."

Bob gave Brenda a frisky grin. "Or maybe you'll come out on my boat, Brenda?"

Brenda playfully laughed and tagged Bob on the arm. "Every day you put a smile on my face. Yell if you need anything else."

Bob watched her give him a little back-side wiggle as she walked away then re-constructed the newspaper tower. *Hello, hello what do we have here?* Bob carefully read the announcement under the *Hip Happenings* section of the paper:

*Newport Historic Society will hold its Annual*

*Flowers in the Moonlight Ball*

*Friday, July 16th*

*At Marble House*

*Attire is black tie. Invitation RSVP must be received by July 5th. All proceeds will benefit the Historic Society.*

Following the announcement was a journalist's commentary about the gala. He scanned over the highlights, *if lucky enough to attend…height of the Newport summer social events…peppered with debutants and grande dames…a most elegant setting for Newport's movers and shakers and the just plain wealthy…* Bob wondered, *why put an announcement out if you need to be invited to get in? Rich people are weird. They want everyone to know what they're doing but they don't want everyone to be a part of it. I bet Maddie Marcelle will be a part.*

Bob picked up his cell phone to finagle an invite. He clicked off the call and set his phone back down next to his breakfast plate. He almost felt bad it was so easy, even pleasurable, to get what he wanted from Maddie. *Upside, I will crack Maddie's shell, probably bang her and meet some new cougars. Downside, I gotta rent a tux.*

# THIRTY-FOUR

A polished black Range Rover rumbled to a stop along Broadway, careful not to park under a street lamp. The only dirt on the SUV was the mud that had been intentionally smeared on the license plate.

Back in the 1970s, Newport was a rough Navy town. Home to dozens of tattoo parlors and bars where bands played in cages for their own protection. Since then Newport had seen a renaissance. Not quite the Gilded Age, but the waterfront revitalization had turned the city into a summer tourist mecca. This stretch of Newport, on the outskirts of the city, was what remained of Newport's seedy past; still dotted with gay clubs, dive bars, and smoke shops.

Even with his hat pulled down, hands in his pockets and head ducked, James Cooper was a striking figure. He quickly walked around a corner toward the back entrance of a massage parlor, unaware of the blonde man watching him from a car that had just rolled up across the street.

As soon as James Cooper had rounded the corner the blonde man hopped from his car and scuttled along the building like a gutter rat. He twitched with anticipation as he watched James Cooper move toward the club he too used to frequent. He wasn't sure if James had seen him. He wasn't quite ready for James to know he had been following and documenting him. He just needed a little more information. Still, he could deliver a powerful blow to James' world, although it wouldn't be as catastrophic as he hoped.

James pulled the bill of his baseball cap lower, he thought he had seen a familiar figure but he needed to keep moving. Time was short. He had a big event to attend with his wife tonight, making it all the more pressing to get his particular needs out of his system. James Cooper hated this side of himself but he also couldn't deny it.

# THIRTY-FIVE

L olly lifted her hair. James allowed the tips of his fingers to graze her shoulders as he pulled the chain up her neck and affixed the clasp. Lolly turned to show off her diamond necklace.

"How do I look?"

"Radiant." James adored his wife. He could never love another woman as much as he loved Lolly. Fortunately, Paris offered more than just women. They were leaving next week for their house in Fontainebleau, close to France's capital city. He would spend his days with his beloved

Lolly and some nights… his thoughts turned dark, *at least the dollar is coming back against the euro*. There would be a premium for the behaviors James favored.

# THIRTY-SIX

B ob swung his Mustang in to the parade of Bentleys, Porches, and limousines turning off Bellevue Avenue and passing through imposing, gilded and black iron gates. He tossed his keys to one of the valets and said, "Watch da paint, 'dose flames are custom."

The valet grinned and nodded, not sure if Bob was kidding or not.

A man with a clipboard was standing, dwarfed by sequoia sized, white marble Corinthian columns, at the entrance to Marble House checking names on a list. Bob chuckled to himself as he approached the man with the clipboard thinking, *at least I don't risk this one sending me to the hospital.*

Bob entered a ballroom and looked around trying to pick Maddie out from a sea full of men dressed like orca whales and women gleaming and turning like colorful fish.

This was a who's who celebration. But even within this niche of wealth there was a pecking order; comprised of grande dames on top all the way down to the want-to-be people looking around for photo opportunities to make it into the social section of the media outlets covering the event.

*Definitely worth the cost of a tux,* Bob thought.

~~~~~~~~~

"Champagne?" A young woman with her hair pulled tight into a bun offered up a silver tray. Kelly, Maddie and Jack retired their empty glasses and replaced them with effervescent new flutes.

"This is by far the most elegant event I have ever attended!" Kelly gushed.

The ballroom dazzled. A beaux arts room encrusted in so much bright gold, to see it felt like looking at the sun.

Jack winked and toasted Kelly with his glass, "Well, just wait until our wedding."

"Your wedding will be beautiful," Maddie chimed in, "but I've got to back Kelly up here. This is a pretty posh event. Those flower arrangements must be more than six feet tall." Maddie looked at Kelly. "Remember how much the arrangements you were looking at cost? What do you think that tower of flower power would set you back?"

"I'm afraid to even guess." Kelly laughed, then noticed Maddie turning to look at the room's entry again. "Hoping to see one of your beaus?" Kelly teased.

"Oh look, there's Bob." Maddie perched up on her toes and waved, hoping to catch Bob's eye.

"Oh, good," Kelly mocked to Jack. "Of the three guys she's seeing, that one has to show up."

Another server veered over with a tray full of savory tidbits and presented them to the group.

"Don't mind if I do," came Bob's voice as he reached around Maddie's back to grab a prosciutto wrapped fig.

"Well, hello!" Maddie smiled and offered her cheek to Bob for a kiss. Instead, he swiped over for a full lip plant.

"Classy," Kelly commented under her breath to Jack.

Maddie waved a hand toward Kelly for a re-introduction. "Kelly, you remember Bob?"

"I do," Kelly said, gently waving her fingers toward him. "Although I wish I couldn't," she added in Jack's ear.

"And this is Jack McCarthy, Kelly's fiancé."

Bob shook hands with Jack. "Quite the shindig huh?" Bob commented, grabbing a glass from a passing tray.

Kelly's disdain for Bob put Jack on alert. He decided to do a little investigating. "So Bob, Maddie tells us you live here in Newport. Do you work here too?"

Bob chugged his champagne like a beer. "My work takes me different places; here, Providence, around."

"And what kind of work is it you do?" Jack continued.

Bob eyed Jack for a quick moment as his mind settled on a plausible lie. "Mostly art. Not like the fancy stuff they got hanging in here, more like contemporary."

Maddie gave Bob a skeptical look. "I didn't know you dealt with art."

"Yeah, an umm, old friend introduced me to it." Bob smirked a little as the inspiration for his career story, Mrs. Vanderbeck, flickered through his thoughts. "So What da you do, Jack?"

"I'm a police detective."

Bob nestled a hand into the small of Maddie's back. He realized he'd have to watch himself around her. *Good to know, gotta go.* "Hey Maddie, the band's playing our song, let's dance."

~~~~~~~~

"You are a surprisingly good dancer, Bob." Maddie commented as Bob swung her around the glossy oak, herringbone-patterned floor.

"Thank you, but why are you surprised?"

Maddie scrunched her brows. "I don't know. I guess every time I think I have you figured out, you do something unexpected." Maddie loved jazz and happily swayed in Bob's arms. His enticing eyes locked on hers as he reeled her in from a twirl.

*Gotcha.* Bob decided to go in for another kiss when he felt a firm tap on his shoulder. He turned to see a strikingly handsome man, ready to square off with him.

"I'm a friend of Madison. My name is Winston Cooper. Hope you don't mind if I cut in?"

Bob silently counted, *one, two, three,* to keep his temper in check. "I guess I'll go get a drink. See ya in a bit, Maddie."

~~~~~~~~

Maddie allowed Winston to gracefully move her around the floor. She tipped her head back, and clung to his tux, so she could admire the baroque ceiling mural. Under the dreamy eyes of cherubs smiling down at her she laughed. "I think I'm happy! Yes, not only am I happy, I'm lucky!"

Winston also smiled down at her. "I'm glad to hear that. Is this a revelation for you, or a champagne induced declaration?"

"Both. I'm taking Kelly's advice and enjoying the moment tonight."

Winston tightened his embrace. "Well, I'm happy I am a part of the moment."

~~~~~~~~

Marble House's huge scaled rooms were designed for entertaining. Bob crossed out of a pink Numidian marble lined room, through substantial carved wood and gilt doors, into the crowded central event space, the great Stair Hall. It was from this enormous Stair Hall that the party stemmed off and spread through several of the mansion's first floor rooms. The airy, ornate, yellow marble and gold Stair Hall shot up two stories high. A cocktail bar spanned the foot of the grand staircase. Bob noted the line at the bar and opted to continue to explore. He entered a dark toned, gothic style room. The blood-red walls of the room emitted a sense of foreboding. Which probably accounted for the virtually unoccupied bar set in a corner with a back drop of stained glass.

*Well this makes everything better,* Bob thought as he approached a woman who looked to be in her late fifties or early-sixties flashing with diamonds pressed up to the corner bar. She held her glass out for a refill from a bartender, smiled at Bob, and strutted away.

"I'll take a whiskey straight up." Bob watched her walk away while he waited for his whiskey. *Some prime, well-aged meat here tonight,* he thought and decided to see where Miss Flashing Diamonds was headed.

~~~~~~~~

"Hey, isn't that Maddie's friend, Bob?" Jack pointed to a man running his index finger over a much older woman's diamond necklace, then re-tracing his finger where the necklace topped her cleavage.

Kelly pulled away from Jack. Jack knew Kelly rarely needed back-up but he quickly followed his fiancé; more afraid of what she would do to Bob than what he would do to her. The older woman hurried away as Jack and Kelly approached.

"Hey, Bob, if you're here with Maddie, shouldn't you be with Maddie?" demanded Kelly.

Bob's olive complexion was turning a shade of crimson. He bowed his head and took a breath before answering. "I was with her. But then a guy named Winston Cooper showed up."

"So, you just decided to play the party field?" Kelly pressed.

"As a matter of fact, yeah I did." He knew it wouldn't be good to pick a fight with the detective's wife. It took every fiber of his being to respond in a civil tone. "I respect that Maddie is honest and told me she is dating a couple of guys right now. I think she would give me the same courtesy. And not for nothing, but what goes on between me and Maddie is none of your business."

Kelly pitched forward toward Bob's face. "You date my friend, and it is my business!"

Jack knew the look on Kelly's face. It meant this discord would only escalate. He stepped between them and interrupted. "You know what, Bob, do what you want to do. Come on, Kelly, we got a wedding coming up. Let's go practice dancing." Jack gently directed Kelly out of the gothic room and back into the ballroom where the jazz band was playing.

~~~~~~~~

Winston kept Maddie close as they swayed to the music. As the song ended he apologized. "I must go over and talk to the Morgans."

"Oh, of course, Winston. There, I see Kelly and Jack. I'll catch up with you later."

Jack saw Maddie approaching before Kelly did. "Kelly, I know you're protective of Maddie." He could tell from her frown he would need to be firm. "She's an adult and she needs to figure out who she wants to spend her personal time with on her own. She's also stubborn, like you, and if you tell her not to see Bob she will do the opposite."

"Damn it!" Kelly knew Jack was right.

"What's wrong?" Maddie laid a caring hand on Kelly's back.

Kelly looked at Jack. He gave her a subtle 'no' shake with his head.

"Nothing." Kelly feigned a smile toward Maddie. "Jack and I were just discussing music selections for the wedding. I think we need to move around. Why don't we go check out the rest of the party?"

"Good work," Jack whispered in Kelly's ear as they moved through the revelers.

"It will be good work if I can show her Bob's true colors. Maybe she'll dump him on the spot," Kelly responded.

~~~~~~~~

"Bit of a crowd at the bar," Kelly observed as they entered the Stair Hall.

"Yes, but it's a great people-watching crowd. I don't mind waiting," Jack answered as they moved toward the bar.

Kelly nodded her head to Jack then turned to see Maddie scanning the palatial hall. "Maybe Jared's here, just in another room," she said into Maddie's ear.

Maddie decided to venture out, leaving Kelly and Jack to order drinks. She wandered past the immense staircase and rounded a barrier of lush potted trees that seemed to have been freshly pulled from the rainforest. In a large alcove created by the overhead stairs she noted another bar with barely a customer waiting. She was about to go back to save Kelly and Jack from the line when she spied Jared.

A row of French doors topped with arched windows stretched up two stories to create a wall of glass that filled the backside of the Stair Hall. A gentle ocean breeze rolled over the sprawling lawn, across the stone veranda, causing gossamer curtains that veiled the open French doors to flutter into the party. Although the music was certainly not as loud here as it had been in the ballroom, Maddie noted Jared was standing very near to a man of similar build and age. Fabric gently billowed around them.

*I wonder who he's with? Something is going on. They're awfully close to each other,* Maddie thought as she approached. She did not want to intrude on their tete-a-tete but curiosity got the best of her. Maddie joined the two men and quietly said, "Hello."

A friendly smile emanated from Jared as he greeted her and made an introduction. "Maddie Marcelle, this is my closest friend in the world and business associate, Ken Tate."

Maddie extended her hand. "That's quite an introduction."

"I would've expected nothing less," Ken said. His tight stare remained on Jared for an extra moment. He turned to Maddie and firmly grasped her hand. "Jared has told me many stories about you. It's good to finally put a face with a name."

"Stories?" Maddie gave Ken an apprehensive shrug. "Nothing too bad, I hope."

"Nothing too bad." Ken's words were innocuous but his eyes said different.

Before the typical discovery of person questions could evolve between Ken and Maddie, another round of introductions was being made as Kelly and Jack had united with the group.

Like a queen holding court all eyes were on Maddie as she delighted the group with genuinely funny stories of house hunting in Newport. Kelly quickly assessed how comfortable and relaxed Maddie seemed around Jared.

"Let's go back to the ballroom, Jack. We can get some more dance practice in for our wedding."

Jack knew this meant Kelly approved of Jared enough to leave Maddie with him.

~~~~~~~~

*This place is great. I friggin' love free booze,* Bob thought as he scouted the crowd from a small bar tucked behind the grand staircase. *There's Miss Maddie. Hanging out with two guys. What are the odds one of those dudes is my competition? Better go check it out.* He took a swig of whiskey and slid away from the bar. "Hey Maddie, remember me?" Bob called out as he sauntered up to the trio gathered by the open French doors.

Her face flushed as she saw Bob grinning at her. *Oh gosh! I knew this was bound to happen. Clash of the dating gladiators.*

Bob extended his hand toward Jared. "I'm just bustin' ya, Maddie. Hey, I'm Bob Lackey. Friend of Maddie's."

Jared shook Bob's hand. "I'm Jared Diamond. Also, a friend of Maddie. This is my friend and business associate, Ken Tate."

Bob squinted intently at Ken. "You look awfully familiar. Do I know you from somewhere?"

Ken laid a hand on Jared's shoulder. "Well it's my friend, Jared, here who graces the covers of magazines. Maybe you saw a tiny photo of me on the 'to be continued' page of an article?"

"Yeah, maybe that's it. Do you work here in Newport? What da ya do?"

Ken quickly tired of answering Bob's questions. *What's with the third degree? And that ill-fitting tux tells me this guy isn't someone I will be doing any business with. Besides I must get to know more about this girl Jared's messing with.*

"If you two will excuse me." Ken offered his forearm up to Maddie. "Perhaps we should get to know each other better. Let's go to the ballroom."

Left alone with Jared, Bob made his plans clear. "This is weird. I'm going to drink more. See ya."

~~~~~~~~

From the moment they faced off on the dance floor Ken peppered Maddie with questions about her and Jared. Just when she thought she could get a word in, he broadened the track of his queries to include other men she might be seeing. "So, I gathered you are also dating Bob. Are you with anyone else, besides Bob and Jared?"

"I don't mean this to sound rude Ken, but I don't think my dating life is any of your business."

"Sorry, I have an inquisitive nature." Ken's lips formed a tight line. "Besides you're such a lovely girl, I just imagine you're not limiting yourself. You're clearly in a position to date any man you want."

Maddie tried to lighten the mood. "Ken, are you asking me out?"

His eyes flashed with disbelief as his body slightly recoiled. "Of course not!"

She had clearly thrown him off and took advantage of the pause in his interrogation. "So, Ken, did you come here with a date?"

Ken looked her in the eye as he answered, "Yes. Jared. We rode over here together."

Maddie's brow furrowed with confusion. "Oh no, I meant is there a special someone in your life?"

"Of course there is." Ken smirked. "Like you, I prefer to keep my private life confidential. I will tell you a little secret. I won't let my special someone be public knowledge, but it is someone the public would know."

~~~~~~~~~

The last note of the music had faded but Ken's words still sounded in Maddie's ear.

"May I have this next dance?" Jared had appeared next to Ken and Maddie.

"I've been waiting all night for you to ask!" exclaimed Ken.

"You're going to have to keep waiting," Jared retorted. "I was speaking to the lady."

Ken winked and squeezed Jared's shoulder. "I'm going to get another drink."

~~~~~~~~

"Busy night for you?" Jared commented as he led Maddie around the dance floor. He tried not to sound snide, but it was difficult.

Maddie stiffened sensing an impending battle of the dating gladiators. Maybe she could play coy a little longer.

"How so?"

"For one thing, I noticed your friend Winston couldn't take his eyes off you while you were dancing with Ken. Don't worry I gave him a little nod before I walked over here."

"Jared, please don't be like that. It's a fundraiser. It has the word 'fun' in it. Let's just have fun tonight."

"Come on, Maddie. I usually welcome competition, but even this is a bit much."

"This is an unusual circumstance, Jared. I enjoy spending time with you, but tonight it's not just about you and me." Maddie rubbed her hands over his shoulders as they danced hoping to assuage his discomfort and not spark a fight on a night when she finally felt so good.

"No. It's also about Winston and Bob," Jared countered.

It had been a long time since Maddie felt in control and confident. She kept her tone friendly as she wanted to handle the situation with care.

"You know, jealousy doesn't go well with your tux tonight." Her attempt to express her feelings in a lighthearted manner fell flat. She halted her dancing feet. *I'm in control,* she thought and this time she really believed it. "In all seriousness, I'm doing my best to be honest with you," she stated in a solemn tone. "I am willing to have this conversation, just not here and now. How about you and I spend all day together tomorrow? Just us, no other guys, no jealousy. Deal?"

~~~~~~~~~

Maddie stuffed her lipstick back into her evening bag. *Better off checking my makeup in the bathroom. Lighting in here is terrible,* she thought as she rose from a scarlet velvet seat that was more of a throne than a chair.

"Hey you," Bob said. He seemed to have materialized out of thin air in front of her.

"Hello. Where did you come from?" Maddie asked, a bit surprised.

"I was over there in the corner, visiting my favorite bar. Never a line. People don't seem to stick around in this red room for very long."

"I can't imagine why," Maddie commented sarcastically.

"Maddie, in case I didn't say it already, I want to thank you for inviting me to this shindig."

Maddie politely smiled.

Bob waved his drink glass in a wide sweep. "Sure are a lot of highfalutin people here. Including your, ah, male friends." Bob put an emphasis on the word 'friends' and gestured big air-quotes with one hand.

Maddie rolled her eyes. "Let's not get into this, Bob. I'm sorry you've had to see me dancing with other guys."

"No, no, no. It really is fine. You told me we're not exclusive. I get that more than anyone." Bob's open body language backed up his words.

"I have a feeling you do, Bob," Maddie responded. *I really am in control,* she thought as Bob continued speaking.

"Maddie, I just want to be sure that I am still in the running with the pretty-boy competition. Besides, this place is a good business opportunity for me."

Maddie gave a sigh of relief. "Well, I'm glad you're not jealous. I'm not looking for a serious relationship right now. And for the record you are included on the dance card both tonight and most likely another night."

Bob was much less concerned about her affection for him and much more curious about her insight on Ken. "Yeah, that's good to hear. So speaking of business, what do you know about that guy Ken?"

Her invisible antennae went up at his question. "Not much. I just met him tonight. I know he's a very good friend of Jared and they're in business together; something with money and computers. Why do you ask?"

"Just curious." He thought quick to extend a more satisfactory answer. "I'm always on the lookout for new business connections." Bob had a nagging feeling he knew Ken. *I just can't place him. I need to go figure this out,* he thought. "If you'll excuse me Maddie, this room feels a bit oppressive."

~~~~~~~~

Kelly pointed Jack in the direction of Maddie and Bob, "Looks like the clown is back and the juggling act continues."

"Yeah, but it seems like they're both doing a juggling act tonight." Jack chuckled.

Kelly did not look amused.

Jack tried to put her at ease. "Don't worry Kelly, Maddie's just having fun. That guy Bob is a player. She'll see right through him. Look, he's walking away from her. Okay, here she comes, remember we're having fun."

Kelly gave Jack an exaggerated toothy grin and turned to greet her friend.

~~~~~~~

Engrossed in the smooth sound of a saxophone, Maddie shifted her shoulders and tapped her foot. She watched her friends move about the dance floor.

"Madison?"

Ken had surfaced next to her. He cast his eyes about the room then discreetly pointed a finger to their right. "Is that James Cooper over there?"

The question felt rhetorical given the expression on Ken's face. Maddie couldn't help but notice the look emanating from Ken's eyes, like a lion in a butcher shop.

Ken reeled in his thoughts before he spoke. "He would be a huge client for my company. Come with me, we'll go introduce ourselves."

Maddie didn't have time to object as Ken grabbed her hand and pulled her through a wake of glimmering dresses.

"James Cooper." Ken's words were an announcement, not a question.

James turned to see Ken beaming at him with an extended hand. "Do I know you?" James asked a bit apprehensively as Ken pressed his hand into Cooper's.

"Well, you do now. Ken Tate. I own Spinnaker Ventures."

James' face changed from an irritated gaze to a knowing smile. "Well, hello. You're Madison Marcelle."

Ken's ire made him immobile. He could only watch as Maddie stepped forward into James' open arms for an embrace.

"I'm James Cooper. My son has shown me photos of you. He has nothing but praise for you. Although he didn't tell me you would be here. I've barely seen him tonight. I suppose he's making the rounds, as we all are. You must come to the house before we leave for Paris so we can get to know you properly. Now, please excuse me. I have a little score to settle with my friend Skipper over there. Do have Winston bring you by soon."

James bent down, placed a gentle peck on Maddie's cheek, stepped away and was swallowed by the crowd.

Ken's face contorted with a look of worry, anger, and hurt.

Maddie felt compelled to say something, anything. "Sorry, Ken I..."

Ken pulled a buzzing phone from his pocket. "I need to take this." He turned and darted away.

~~~~~~~~~~

Ken swiftly moved to a less public spot where he could read the text that had just come through on his covert line. The message read, *What the hell do you think you're doing?*

Ken clicked an answer back, *Enjoying the party. Same as you!* He slipped the phone back into his left pocket.

~~~~~~~~

"Sorry I haven't been more attentive, darling." Winston appeared at Maddie's side. "I saw you but I wasn't able to get to you in time. It looked like you met my father? I hope he didn't say anything to scare you off?"

"No, not at all, he told me you've only said wonderful things about me and that I should have you bring me around so we can get to know each other properly."

Winston kissed Maddie's cheek. "Of course, my dear. I know you want to take things slowly. So when you're ready I will drop you into the shark tank. It seems you made a new friend too. That man you were dancing with, the one who was standing with you and my father, is he a friend of yours or my father's?"

"Honestly, I just met him tonight. Although, your father seemed to look at him as if he knew him but once Ken introduced himself he didn't seem to know him at all. I felt awful because I thought Ken wanted to talk a little business with him, but your dad spotted me and acted like Ken wasn't even standing there."

"Ken?" Winston pressed for more information. "So not a friend of yours but you were dancing with him?"

"Are you jealous?" Maddie teased but hoped his answer would not put her on defense.

"Madison, I don't think I have anything to be jealous about. I'm just inquiring because I care about you."

"I know, Winston," she answered with a slight sigh of relief. "His name is Ken Tate. I didn't want to bring it up, but I met him through Jared. They're friends and have business ties."

Winston looked over Maddie's shoulder and across the room. "I see. What a small world." He looked back down towards Maddie. "Please forgive me, I must excuse myself. I see the Montgomerys are here and they are instrumental to one of my charities. It seems managing people tonight is turning into quite a job for me."

~~~~~~~~~

Jared felt vibrations running through the side of his tux. *Damn it. Too many pockets in this thing. Which one has the phone?* He tapped around his jacket then reached deep into the right side of his coat. "Hey, Charlie. Are you sure? Are you absolutely sure it wasn't Shane or anyone else in accounting? Shit! I can't believe this! No, no, I gotta go." Jared desperately craned his head around the room. *Where the hell is Ken?*

~~~~~~~~~

The phone in Ken's left pocket buzzed again with a text message: *Meet me outside in the pagoda. I must talk to you right now!*

126

A few seconds later the phone in Ken's right pocket buzzed with a call. Ken darted to a quieter space and leaned against a high-top party table covered with white linen and flowers as he spoke on the phone.

Bob was approaching Ken from behind. He was just steps away from his encounter when Ken turned his head over his shoulder and Bob overheard him as he finished his phone call.

"I'll keep you posted. Don't worry, I'll let you know when it's done," Ken said into the phone.

Bob suddenly halted as if he had slammed into an invisible brick wall. He knew where he had seen Ken. The day he had to grovel for a financial extension at Cosimo DeCastelleri's office. Ken was the blonde man in the hall.

~~~~~~~~~

Bob moved in like a hunter closing on his prey to confront Ken. "It seems we have a mutual friend," Bob spoke with a sly confidence.

The blonde man gave him doubtful look. "Oh, yeah, who's that?"

Bob inched a bit closer. Years of poker playing had trained Bob to watch for subtle reactions. "I know you're working on a project for Cosimo DeCastelleri. I've seen you in his office."

Ken seemed calm, but for a brief widening of his eyes. *Gotcha!* Bob thought.

"I work with a lot of business owners. It's what I do," Ken said collectedly.

"Yeah, save it Ken. I just want in on the deal with Cosimo."

Ken looked annoyed. Yet again, evenly replied, "I don't know what you're talking about."

But Bob Lackey was like a dog with a bone and persisted. "Maybe if I go and tell your big wig friend, Jared, about you and your association with Mr. D., I'd bet he'd be real interested in your ties."

Ken lurched forward to Bob's ear, so his sharp message could be heard clearly. "Really? How do you know Jared isn't involved too? Back off asshole!" Ken's shoulder jammed into Bob as he pushed past him, headed toward the back of the Stair Hall.

*That's the temper of a guilty man and it takes one to know one. Weasel. You're not getting off this easy,* Bob thought. He was flustered by his encounter with Ken but before he made any accusations that could blow up in his face, he needed to find out if Jared was involved with the organization too. Bob had a plan, *time for a run in with Jared.*

~~~~~~~~

Jared looked down at his phone again. No response. He slid his phone back into the side pocket of his tux jacket just as he spotted Ken moving from the bar behind the grand staircase. He was so focused on reaching Ken he did not see Bob until after he mowed into him.

"Sorry, Jared," Bob apologized.

"It's fine," Jared muttered. His eyes fixed on Ken. "I gotta go." He swiftly pushed forward through the throng of guests.

~~~~~~~~

Jared's face was flush with emotion. "I need to talk to you right now," he demanded.

"What's this about?" Ken was clearly irked by Jared's confrontation.

"You know what this is about. It's about money. But mostly it's about betrayal."

Ken angled his face next to Jared's ear. "Not here. Look around. We can talk in private."

An evening of whiskey drinking had done its part to intensify Jared's reactions. His voice was an angry sob. "I thought we were a team!" He snagged up the left lapel of Ken's tuxedo. "After everything we have been through together."

Ken tried to break free of Jared's grip but Jared would not yield, causing Ken's jacket to be yanked half off of him. Ken shoved Jared backward with his free hand and shook his half-removed jacket back onto his arm.

The surrounding party guests began taking notice of their brawl.

"Stop it Jared," Ken growled. "We are not doing this here." Ken abruptly turned and cut a path toward the wall of French doors open to the outdoor veranda.

"Don't you walk away from me!" Jared angrily spewed. "This isn't over Ken, this is far from over!"

Jared looked around, his wild eyes suddenly aware of guests staring at him. He dropped his head and ran his hands along sides of his hair. As he looked down he noticed a phone on the floor. He ducked his hands into his jacket, empty. *Damn it, I must have dropped it dealing with Ken.* He picked up the phone and absently allowed it to slide deep into an interior pocket of his tux. At that moment a hand clamped on his raised elbow. Maddie pulled his arm forcing Jared to spin around and look at her.

Her eyes swept the space behind Jared looking for Ken as she questioned, "What's going on?"

~~~~~~~~

*Damn.* Bob finished scrolling through the phone he had lifted off Jared after he plowed into him. None of Jared's calls, contacts or texts seemed to have any connection to Cosimo DeCastelleri. He was slinking his way back through the bustling Stair Hall when he spied Ken a few steps ahead of him.

Ken was headed toward a tall French door open to the night air. *Where do you think you're going, you little weasel?* Bob deftly side stepped his way through the crowd to close in on Ken. *That's right, go outside so I can get you alone. I've got you now,* Bob thought as he followed Ken outside onto the stone terrace.

~~~~~~~~

Jared was still looking down, shaking his head in frustration when Maddie saw Ken pass outside through one of the large glass doors leading out to the stone veranda, followed immediately by Bob.

"Maddie, I know you mean well. But I can't talk about this right now. I'm furious. I need answers and I need to get some air. Alone. Please, I just need a little time."

Maddie had no time to respond as Jared's lips brushed her cheek and he quickly peeled away into the crowd.

She felt as if someone had reached down her throat, grabbed her stomach and twisted it into their fist. She really did care about this man.

~~~~~~~~~

Bob watched Ken's shadow fuse with the night as Ken headed toward the Chinese pagoda at the north corner of the estate. No lights down that far on the property; just a shimmer of moonlight when the clouds parted indicating the dark outline of a structure against an almost charcoal colored sky. *Perfect*, thought Bob. *Take your time. I'll take mine, cause now I've got you all to myself.*

Bob knew he needed to stay calm. He moved into the deeper darkness provided by an enormous weeping beech tree. He leaned against the massive gnarled trunk and pulled out a cigarette. He was careful to keep his hand over the ash ember, so as not to give away his position.

~~~~~~~~~

"It just doesn't sit right with me," Maddie declared. "I want to help out. I mean, I know how I would feel if you and I had a fight." She looked at Kelly for affirmation.

"I get it Maddie." Kelly gave her friend a welcome embrace. "What were they fighting about anyway?"

"I don't have the details but Jared had alluded to some money problems at his company. And I know Ken is his business something or other, like a financial guy."

"Maddie, if I can give you some advice?" Jack spoke up, then answered his own rhetorical question. "Whatever that fight was about, Jared is one pissed off dude. If he says he needs some time to cool down, then just take him at his word and give him some space."

Kelly joined rank with her fiancé adding, "Please Maddie, Jack has a point. Just try to let it go."

Maddie let out a deep breath as she caved to their reasoning.

~~~~~~~~~

Ken climbed the wide, wooden steps of the pagoda style Tea House. He pushed the front door which gave way with a creak. Inside was completely dark, but for shadows from the half moon shining through windows facing the water.

"Anyone in here?" called Ken as he ventured further into the house.

"It's time we talk about what's going on," came the answer.

Ken stepped forward toward the voice. "Are you sure all you want to do is talk?" Ken asked seductively.

"No, that's not all I want," was the response.

Cool hands were suddenly around Ken's neck, squeezing harder and tighter. Ken flailed his arms, reaching, scratching the tuxedo material of his attacker. Ken tried to yell but only garbled chokes came out.

"I didn't want to hurt you, Ken. I never wanted this to happen." His arms and knuckles ached from the pressure he was exerting onto Ken's throat. "But I trusted you. I told you I was dead serious about protecting this part of my life. Now you're making me do this. I have to do this before you ruin everything!"

The panic and pain were too much. Ken couldn't fight anymore. He tried to focus as a pale glint of moonlight illuminated the gritted, barred teeth of his attacker. It was the last thing he ever saw.

"We should've had more time together," the killer whispered as he searched Ken's pockets. He removed Ken's cell phone, then froze a moment. *Footsteps? No, my imagination. Probably surf on the rocks. I must get out of here.* He crept to a back door and silently exited. He crossed out onto the bridge over Cliff Walk, wound his arm back and hurled the phone far over the jagged rocks into the ocean.

A few moments later a black, patent leather shoe made contact with Ken's ribs. Nothing. The shoe prodded again. Still no movement. *Weasel.* He pivoted his black, patent leather shoes and retreated back through the door from which he came.

~~~~~~~~

*Oh, thank God. There he is.* Maddie was finally able to lay eyes on Jared. He was propped up on the corner of a bar and still seemed rattled as she laid a hand on his arm. "Do you want to talk about what happened with Ken?"

Jared's glassy eyes flared with clarity as he emphatically answered, "No!"

Bob saw Maddie approach Jared. *Perfect timing,* he thought as he quickly and effectively stumbled into Jared, causing Jared to turn and push Bob backward. The distraction worked. Bob slipped Jared's phone back into a jacket pocket on Jared's right side.

"Hey there, I really like this tune Maddie, you wanna dance?" asked Bob.

Maddie sensed Jared really needed a friend right now, whether he wanted to talk or not. She jumped in before Jared could answer for her. "I'm sorry, Bob, we need to finish our conversation. I'll find you later."

"No problem," Bob answered. *Besides, my work here is done.*

~~~~~~~~

Winston adjusted his tie and smoothed his jacket. *Not the night I expected to say the least.* He watched the scene playout between Bob, Jared and Maddie. He was annoyed but now was not the time to deal with Jared. His eyes followed Bob as he walked away from the pair. *Well at least he doesn't seem to be someone I need to worry about.*

~~~~~~~~

Maddie again placed her hand gently on Jared's forearm. "Jared, I know you don't want to talk—"

"Yeah, I don't want to talk. The person I needed to talk to was Ken, but he's not talking to me." Jared jerked his arm away from Maddie's grasp. "I had some bad news about our business. Obviously, I didn't handle the situation well but I've had a few drinks," he snarled.

Maddie had never seen Jared act this cold, but she desperately wanted to help him. She continued to tread lightly, "I know you're upset..."

Jared stepped back from her before she could finish speaking. His sharp tone had dulled. "I might have had too much to drink. I'm gonna go use the restroom and then I think I gotta get out here. I'm sorry. I'll talk to you tomorrow." He immediately pivoted and strode away.

~~~~~~~~

"Oh, there you are, love!" Lolly exclaimed as she hooked her arm around James Cooper's elbow. "Where have you been?"

"Sorry, dear, I was making the rounds. Listen, I've got a screaming headache starting. I think it best to leave now."

"Of course, my love, you look quite pale. Let's get you home".

In an odd role reversal, Lolly was the one holding James steady as she steered the couple out the front doors.

~~~~~~~~

Bob promptly made his way to the front hall to exit. *That's enough of this shit,* he thought as he gave his ticket to the valet. *After what happened in that pagoda, it's time to get the hell out of here.*

~~~~~~~~

"Help! There's a body! He's not moving!" A young man and woman were rushing over the grass toward the stone terrace waving their arms.

Maddie snagged Kelly's arm as Jack bolted out the open French door toward the screams for help. Kelly broke free, chasing Jack with Maddie just behind her.

As he approached the couple, Jack called out, "I'm a police officer. I can help you."

Panting with distress the girl exclaimed, "There, down there." She waved her arm toward the ocean.

The young man interjected to clarify, "In that little house. There's a guy, on the floor, we tried to wake him up, but he's not moving. Something's wrong."

~~~~~~~~

135

Maddie was through the door of the pagoda first and quickly found where the body was lying. Her nursing skills kicked in as she dropped to a crouch and placed her index and middle finger on his carotid artery. No pulse. She looked up at the stunned faces of both Jack and Kelly and confirmed, "It's Ken Tate and he's dead."

~~~~~~~~

Jack had called for backup and the crime scene unit. He knew he needed to secure the area and would need any available resource.

Jack firmly placed his hands on Kelly's shoulders. "Go find the head of the catering staff. Tell her who I am and that we need all hands on deck to secure the house. No one can leave. Tell her there is no need to panic, but there is a safety issue and the police are on the way. That's all you know. Go." Then he turned to Maddie. "Go find who's in charge of this event and tell them the same thing I told Kelly. I'm going to make an announcement."

~~~~~~~~

Jack flipped the badge in his wallet as he stepped in front of the band and signaled for them to stop playing. "Good evening, everyone. I need your attention please. My name is Jack McCarthy. I'm a detective with the Newport police department. We have a safety issue OUTSIDE of this house. We need you to stay calm and stay inside this house."

The murmur of the crowd began to overpower Jack's message. His voice grew louder as he continued. "Most of all I need for you to stop talking and listen so we can move forward safely here!"

Like the quiet before a storm the crowd fell silent, then a fusillade of questions started.

"What do you mean by safety issue?"

"Should we call our families?"

"What's going on?"

"Is it terrorists?"

Jack held up his hands and tried to address the concerns before a rushed panic set in. Even if he had to lie, calming the crowd and securing the crime scene were his top priorities. "There are NO terrorists. There was someone seriously injured outside, on the property of this house. Newport police are on the way. This appears to be an isolated incident. But to ensure your safety before you can leave we must ask you a few questions. Just to see if you saw anything to help us understand what happened outside and to be sure that no harm will come to you outside of this event.

"Why would harm come to us?" a voice called from the crowd.

Followed by another voice. "Tell us what kind of injury!"

The welcome sight of uniformed officers began to fill the perimeter of the room. Police Captain Larry Todd made his way to the microphone followed by Betsy Cavendish, the event organizer.

Larry gave Jack a nod and added, "Good job, Jack. Your fiancé filled me in. I'll take it from here with the crowd. Go get your people set up to take statements and clear people to leave."

"Alright, Captain. Is CSU here yet?"

"They were right behind me. Your fiancé's friend who touched the body, Marcelle, was working with them."

"Thanks, Captain. I'll coordinate with them too." Jack took a deep breath and headed out through the crowd.

This was not Captain Larry Todd's first murder investigation and certainly not his first time diffusing a crowd. Jack did the right thing to start the process, affirming Larry's decision to move him up to a detective. He just never thought Jack's first big case would be a murder.

~~~~~~~~

Jack jotted down a few more words. "Jared, I know you're anxious to get out of here. Just a couple more questions."

"Look, Jack, my business partner, my best friend was just killed. I need some time to process this. I've told you everything I can remember. I'll come into the station in the morning and go over everything again with you, but I can't take any more."

"Fine, you can go. I'll see you tomorrow. This is my direct line." Jack handed a card to Jared.

Kelly looked around the lavish ballroom the crowd had been divided into groups offering up accounts of what they saw or did not see to officers quickly tapping the information into tablets and scratching notes on paper. She shook her head as she spoke to Maddie. "I can't believe this is happening. Are you okay? I mean, we found Ken dead!"

"Oddly enough, I'm just numb. When I saw Ken lying there, it was like I was on auto-pilot. I was ready to give him CPR, but it was too late."

"Look Maddie, Jack already took our statements and he's going to be here a while. There's not much we can do now. Why don't we get out of here and I'll drop you off at home."

"Alright, but I feel like I should try to find Winston or Jared, and whatever happened to Bob?"

"Winston is over there, in the corner, between the police and the paparazzi. You should just call him tomorrow. Kelly craned her neck around the room, God only knows where Bob is. Hey, here comes Jared."

Maddie stepped in front of Jared. "Hey, what can I do to help you?"

Jared barely looked up. His wet, bloodshot eyes looked like a dam ready to overflow. "I can't do this right now. Please, Maddie, I just need to be alone I'll call you tomorrow."

Maddie stepped aside and nodded. "Okay, whatever you need."

Kelly's arm slid around Maddie's shoulders as they watched Jared tumble away to the exit. "Come on, let's get out of here."

# THIRTY-SEVEN

Jared's body was on auto-pilot. His mind repeated a loop of surreal affirmations that tonight's events did not actually take place. He looked around his office. He didn't remember the drive to get there. He pulled open his closet and mindlessly fumbled the buttons on his tuxedo. He hung it as best he could on the wooden hangers, then exchanged his formal wear for a polo shirt and a pair of jeans.

He poured a strong drink and opened the computer on his desk. There was a photo of Ken and him on a fishing trip. The dam broke. His chest heaved. Tears flooded hot and fast down his face. He sobbed until his bleary eyes finally grew so heavy he allowed his head to rest on his desk. He slipped into a black slumber.

# THIRTY-EIGHT

Captain Larry Todd opened his office door and listened as Jack gave orders to a team of officers assembled in front of Jack's desk.

"Get me anyone who was there with the press. I want photos, notes, everything they have. And we're gonna need to talk to the catering staff, bartenders, door men, valets anyone that was there last night that hasn't finished giving us a statement. We've got a pretty good timeline of our victim's movements, thanks to the fight he had with Jared Diamond, but someone must have seen something more."

Captain Todd stepped out from his doorway and beckoned with his hand, "Detective McCarthy, a word please."

Jack headed into the Captain's office.

"You stepped up to the plate last night, McCarthy. Did you get any sleep?"

Jack shrugged. "A little."

"Understandable. Where do we stand right now?"

"We just got in a list of all the guests. We've finished taking most of their statements and we're working on narrowing down who may need to come back in to help us firm up our victim's movements, how he ended up in the pagoda tea house and who he was with."

"You're on the right track, Jack. Do some digging into our victim too, we need a complete picture of this guy to find out why someone would want him dead."

~~~~~~~~

Jack McCarthy took a deep breath as he ran his hands over an old metal desk that was new to him. He sat down and opened up the murder case file in front of him and pulled out the CSU photos. He corroborated his own experiences last night at Marble House with the accounts from other party goers.

Many people remembered Ken heading outside, alone, then nothing. Jared Diamond, the only person Ken seemed to know at that party, was the best person to shed some light on Ken's murder and at worst, his killer.

# THIRTY-NINE

*D*amn it! *What the hell is going on?* Bob tried a third time to call Cosimo DeCastelleri, only to get the same 'this number is no longer in service' message. He'd just settled into his booth at Gary's Greasy Spoon with the Sunday paper headline announcing Ken Tate's murder. It wasn't news to him but it forced him to scrap his plans of leisure and start tracking down Mr. D.

He re-read the front page article but details were light on the actual murder. The newspaper spin was about the impact of this shocking crime on tourism and the social scene. *I know that weasel Ken Tate was doing something for Mr. D. I was stupid to rush things. I know I could've gotten more information out of him. That doesn't matter now. I'm a betting man, and I bet I can figure out how to make this guy's unfortunate accident work for me. Stupid phone. I gotta go talk to Mr. D.*

~~~~~~~~~~

Traffic was light as Bob headed up route 195 from Newport to Providence. His calls to Mr. D still weren't going through. *Why the hell can't I get ahold of him? He can't just cut me off. Bet he won't be so quick to ignore me once I prove I can handle business.*

~~~~~~~~~~

Bob cruised through DePasquale Square and pushed a buzzer on the black door. He heard the lock click and stepped inside. Before he could ascend the stairs, he walked into a wall of muscle.

"Where you goin'?" the hulking figure asked.

"I gotta see Mr. D," Bob answered.

"I gotta get some identification. What's ya number?"

"It's two, three, four. Look, tell him it's Bob Lackey."

The hulking figure tipped his head to assess Bob. He certainly wasn't in any hurry to alert Mr. D that he had a guest waiting.

"Hey, I got important business to discuss with him. Go tell him." Bob knew his insistence was pushing the boundaries but he was sure Mr. D would find his news about Ken Tate interesting. Bob anxiously shifted his weight from one foot to the other as he tried to look up the staircase beyond the hulking guard.

At the top of the stairs a shadow figure appeared and called down. "It's okay. Let him up."

Bob gave a satisfied grin to the hulk who had stepped away like a door swinging on a hinge.

The shadow figure greeted Bob at the top of the landing and motioned him to follow into Mr. D's office. Bob followed and sat down across from a heavy wooden desk. Mikey, Mr. D's *consigliere* or right-hand man, was sitting in Mr. D's chair. He leaned across the desk and addressed Bob. "Why are you here, Mr. Lackey?"

"Like I said downstairs, I'm here to see Mr. D. Where is he?"

Mikey pushed his substantial body backwards causing the leather chair to crackle as it tilted away from the desk. "Mr. Lackey, Mr. DeCastelleri has made it clear to me that your intellect is in a severe deficit. Now, I am gonna take that into account and assume that what appears to be a lack of respect for this office is in fact just your stupidity."

Bob knew he needed to get in control. His glance darted around the room then rested on the tops of his shoes. *One, two, three, four. Respect, control, respect, control.* He quickly calmed himself and looked up to meet Mikey's eyes. "I apologize for my behavior. I am just surprised not to see Mr. D. I did not mean any disrespect to you, Mikey, or to this office."

Mikey seemed appeased with this answer. "Mr. D is out of the country. He is taking care of some personal family business."

Bob did his best to sound humble and not annoyed. "Oh, I see. I'm sorry to bother you here, in person. It's just that I've tried calling the number I have for Mr. D and I get a disconnected message."

"Right. See, Bob, we've had a potential breech of Mr. DeCastelleri's private numbers. So, all lines to Mr. D have been cancelled. We are currently in the process of issuing new contact information for Mr. DeCastelleri. Starting of course with our priority people." Mikey's hard stare conveyed his next thought without a word, *and you, Bob, are not even close to a priority.*

"Okay. Well I need to talk to Mr. D about Ken Tate." Bob watched Mikey closely to see if the name would illicit a reaction. *Slight eyebrow twitch. Yes!*

"Alright Mr. Lackey. I will convey the message."

"When will I get to talk to him?" Bob blurted out. The narrowing of Mikey's eyes made him add, "I mean assuming all goes well with his personal stuff, about when do you think I might be able to discuss the Ken Tate matter?"

"We'll text you a new number for Mr. DeCastelleri and let you know when you can have an appointment. Freddy will see you to the stairs now."

# Forty

Maddie continued past the service counter at the Ocean Roasters café and took a seat opposite Jared. She took in his pale countenance, and disheveled clothing.

"Have you been able to sleep?" she quietly asked.

"Not really. But I've been thinking..." he stared back down into his coffee cup.

Maddie patiently waited for him to gather his thoughts.

Finally, he continued, "I want to have a memorial service for Ken. It's the least I can do... since this is all my fault."

"Okay. I can help you with a service but how is any of this your fault?"

Jared had buried his face down into his hands.

"Listen, Jared, if there is something you need to tell me, I promise I will do whatever I can to help you. My friend, Jack, is the lead detective on this case. He can get you the best deal possible."

"What?" Jared raised his face up and shook his head in disbelief. "Do you think I killed my best friend?"

Maddie was just as surprised at her own words and stammered, "I don't know. It's just you seem so..."

"Guilty? I am guilty. I'm guilty of bringing him to that damn party. I'm guilty of fighting with him." Jared's cheeks flushed. His eyes had become glossy and wet. "I'm guilty of trusting him. I'm guilty of being angry that I will not get answers to questions I want answered. And if you think I am guilty of murder, then why are you even sitting here with me?"

Maddie recognized the raw emotion in Jared's eyes. She had seen it in the mirror after she lost Mr. Whitmore. She formed a deliberate thought and delivered it slowly. "I don't think you are a killer. I think you are distraught, as you should be, and I apologize for even suggesting anything else. Please, Jared, I know what it is like to lose someone very close to you. I want to help you through this." She laid her hands over his.

Her hands looked so small but felt so warm. He felt their warmth radiating out to his fingertips and closed his eyes. *I can do this,* he thought.

# FORTY-ONE

B ob's mustang rumbled past the police station and pulled into a spot marked for visitors. *Friggin' police. Nothing routine about their questions. I got questions too. But that little prick really pissed me off. Just wish I had taken my time and gotten more information out of that little weasel before he died.*

Jack McCarthy escorted Bob into a small room the department called 'the fishbowl' as two of the room's four walls were comprised of windows which met at a right angle.

"Thank you for coming in Mr. Lackey." Jack directed Bob toward one of four chairs set around a narrow, rectangular, black wooden table. He waited for Bob to take a seat then took up a position across the table from him. Jack opened a manila file folder, clicked the top of a pen, and addressed Bob. "As I said on the phone, we're taking statements from attendees of the Historic Society gala. I noticed that although you were at the event, you haven't given an account of the evening yet."

Bob crossed his arms over his chest before he spoke. "Ok, what do you want to know?"

"I understand you drive a very distinctive car, Mr. Lackey."

Bob gave a brief chuckle. "Yeah, distinctive and distinguished. Why? This Ken guy get run over or something?"

"No." Jack tilted the manila folder up, so its contents were not visible to Bob. "A valet confirms that you left the party before the police were called to the scene of the crime."

149

Bob shrugged. His arms still folded but his tone a bit more defensive. "So? Is it a crime to leave a party?"

"Of course not, Mr. Lackey. I'm just trying to create a timeline with anyone who might have seen Ken. So what time did you leave the party?"

"I don't know. Whatever time the valet says I did."

Jack flipped through a couple pages in the folder. He quickly scanned a statement from Maddie. His eyes settled on the information he wanted. "Did you have any interaction with Ken Tate?"

Bob looked around the room as if he was searching for an answer. "Look, I never met this guy, Ken, before. So any interactions I had were all because your friend Maddie introduced us."

"Okay Mr. Lackey. So I have a witness who gave an account of you asking some questions about Ken. Can you elaborate on your interest in Ken Tate?"

"My interest in asking about Ken Tate is that I'm a business guy. I heard he was a business guy. So, I had a potential business interest in Ken Tate." Bob gave Jack a very satisfactory grin.

"Did your business interest extend to following him and interacting with him outside, just prior to his death?"

"No," Bob was quick to answer.

"See, I also have a witness who saw you go outside directly behind Ken Tate close to the time period we have assigned to his dying."

Bob cast looks around the fishbowl room again. He was not so quick to answer this time. "Yeah, I did go outside. I'm a smoker. I went out a few times that night to have a butt. If I happened to go out at the same time as Ken Tate, it was pure coincidence."

Jack McCarthy studied his file folder another minute. *Either this guy is telling the truth or he can think on his feet. Doesn't matter. I've got nothing else to throw at him right now.* "Thank you for coming in Mr. Lackey."

# FORTY-TWO

Officer Sanders tapped his index finger on Jack's metal desk. "Medical examiner is here with the autopsy report."

Jack stood up, grabbed his file folder and a pen. "Great. Let's go into the fishbowl."

The medical examiner arranged her photographs along the length of the black wooden table. "So, Detective McCarthy and Officer Sanders, here's what we've got. Time of death between 10:30 p.m. and 11:00 p.m. Cause of death, strangulation. Technically his trachea was crushed, along with a cervical vertebra."

The medical examiner pointed to a photograph of Ken Tate's purple and black discolored throat. "See the bruising on the neck is consistent with a manual strangulation. No ligature used. Also, the bruising pattern indicates the victim struggled."

"So, is it possible to get fingerprints from his neck?" Jack asked.

The medical examiner took in a deep breath. "Well, if your killer wore gloves then we won't get anything."

"Talk about pre-meditation," Officer Sanders chimed in. "I mean gloves on a hot summer night?"

"Right," the medical examiner nodded. "So bare hands leave us with a good news, bad news situation."

Jack perked up and encouraged, "Go on."

"So, the good news is that it was a humid night. Which can be useful to trigger latent, invisible prints." The examiner again waved her hand toward a close-up picture of Ken Tate's neck. She had Jack and

Sanders' full attention. "So latent prints can be reproduced from moisture ridges left behind from finger prints." Before Jack or Officer Sanders could speak, she held up a cautionary hand. "However, while it is possible to get a print it is very difficult to get a clean print. Bear in mind that prints can be lost during a struggle, dirt can contaminate the prints, plus a variety of other factors including the victim's own sweat can ruin prints. So, I'm telling you it's a long shot but we can try."

"Okay. What else did you get?" Jack asked.

The examiner scanned her notes. "There's no skin under the victim's nails. So he didn't catch his killer's skin, but there were some fibers. I'm running a search right now to get you some specifics." The examiner walked to the end of the table and pointed to another photo on display. "The bruising on the knees indicates he fell down hard, probably while fighting. There were some hairs on the victim's jacket that didn't belong to him, but it's inconclusive as they could belong to anyone at the event that night not just your killer."

Jack continued to take in the photos as he asked, "What about the tox screen?"

The medical examiner shuffled to another page of her notes. "Right. Toxicology report indicates presence of alcohol but not enough to be over the legal limit and there were no drugs in his system, legal or illegal."

Jack paced around the table absorbing each photo before he spoke. "So we know our killer was big enough to overpower our victim. We are assuming a man."

Officer Sanders gave an affirmative nod, knowing this was a statement not a question.

Jack circled back to a photo of Ken Tate's throat. "But this method of murder is personal, almost intimate." He ran his hand over the neck in the photo. "As opposed to a gunshot it's literally a hands-on, physical connection. This type of killing is a commitment. It's not over fast. It requires struggle, strength, and time." Jack's observations quietly hung in the room for a moment.

Officer Sanders spoke up, "Well my money is on this being an impulsive act. A crime of passion, if you will. The killer may not have planned to murder Ken Tate that night. Perhaps something at the party set our killer off?"

~~~~~~~

Jack sat on the edge of a chair in Captain Larry Todd's office. "We have a pretty good time line for Ken Tate's movements the night of the party, and who he had contact with, sir."

Captain Todd nodded his approval. "Go on."

"The point of contact that stands out is our victim's fight with Jared Diamond. I've interviewed Diamond a couple of times now. He maintains they had a fight over some missing money from his business but after the fight he claims he never saw Ken again."

"Do you believe him?" Captain Todd asked

Jack blew out a sigh. "Here's the thing, I might have a conflict of interest clouding my judgement."

Captain Todd's brow furrowed as he quizzed, "How so?"

"My fiancé's best friend, Maddie, who's my friend too is actually dating Jared Diamond." Jack watched as the Captain processed this information.

The deep eleven's between the Captain's brows smoothed out. He pursed his lips into a pucker before he relaxed them and spoke. "First off Jack, I've been watching you from the start of this investigation and your judgement seems very clear. Second, don't view

154

this as a conflict but rather a way to get more information. Think about it, if you have access to Diamond in a casual setting you can earn his trust. He might let out much more information than he would ever give up in a formal police setting."

"Captain with all due respect if this guy is our killer, I don't want him anywhere near my fiancé or our friend."

"That's a good point Jack, but you're a smart man, you're a good cop. I think you can assess the situation, protect your family and friend, and protect the integrity of this investigation. Use your unique position to keep a close eye on this guy."

Jack dropped his gaze to the floor and rubbed his forehead. "You're right. I'm in a better position to protect the people I care about and move the investigation along if I keep this guy close."

# FORTY-THREE

James Cooper surveyed a collection of car keys hanging on hooks. He bypassed the keys to his Bentley opting for his usual incognito vehicle, Winston's black Range Rover.

Although the Range Rover's blackout windows hid him, James instinctively ducked his head as he recognized Madison Marcelle running towards the steps of St. Joseph's church. He traveled one more block then turned his car sharply to the right off of Broadway. He eased the SUV into a spot between the club's back door and a dumpster which, as it always had in the past, provided complete cover from the street.

~~~~~~~~

Sarah Byron knew Ken wasn't a very nice guy. In fact, he could be downright cruel. Still, she couldn't believe he was dead. Sarah was an avid reader of the Newport News obituaries. One of her favorite hobbies was to attend funeral and memorial services, partly because she liked to get dressed up. Partly since it was such an emotional time it made her feel like a real friend when she could comfort someone in their time of need. As luck would have it, she actually knew Ken. *This one will be special,* she thought as she tugged down on the netting of her purple felt hat.

~~~~~~~~

Sarah took up her usual seat, always the last pew nearest to the door. She looked at the mourners there to pay their respect. She recognized Jared Diamond up in the first pew where the family would normally be seated.

*So weird,* Maddie thought. *That looked like Winston's car. I didn't notice the plate though and besides, what would he be doing around here? He didn't even know Ken Tate. Oh gosh, I can't believe I'm so late to this!* Maddie ran up the steps and crept into the church where the service had already started. She had told Jared she would meet him there but since he was up in the first pew she thought it best to just catch up to him on the way out. She looked around to see if she recognized anyone from the gala. Maybe someone who might be a lead to what happened to Ken. Mostly what she noticed was the sparse number of people in attendance. She ducked into the last pew near the door.

Sarah Byron gave her a smile, then slid closer to Maddie so they could talk. She leaned close to Maddie's face and whispered, "Hi. I'm Sarah." Sarah could barely contain her excitement for the chance to talk about Ken. She explained she worked in the same office building as the deceased.

Maddie scooted a couple inches toward the armrest at the end of the pew to reclaim some of the personal space Sarah had invaded. She could feel Sarah staring at her but she refused to make eye contact. Instead, she focused on the soprano singer at the front of the church belting out a hymnal.

Aloof to social cues, Sarah's chatter was undeterred. She confessed to Maddie one of the reasons she came to the service for Ken was she was hoping to see if there was anyone who thought he might have been a nice person.

Now she had Maddie's attention. "What do you mean by that?" Maddie asked while keeping her gaze fixed on the singer.

Sarah described how they would run into each other in the lobby or the elevator, and how sometimes his mail would end up in her office. "I went out of my way to be friendly to him. But he always seemed annoyed with me. Not at all like when I would see him with his buddy Jared Diamond."

Maddie turned to face Sarah as she continued to talk. "See the guy sitting up there in the front row?" Sarah pointed with her index finger. "You can't miss him. He's the only one up there other than the altar boy. He's super cute and very rich."

"How do you know Jared?" Maddie asked.

"Oh, I don't. I mean I've seen him at the office but I only know what I've read in the magazines or seen on TV. Still, I'm very perceptive and I can just tell he's a good person. In fact, he's the reason I thought Ken might be a decent guy. I would see them together leaving our building for lunch, or wherever it was they went. He and Ken were always laughing and smiling. Made me think Ken must have a fun side."

The service ended. Jared was the first person to solemnly proceed down the aisle. Maddie quickly stepped out and joined pace behind him having determined her gossipy pew mate had nothing more to contribute to her inquiry of what happened to Ken other than that he wasn't very nice and he wasn't very popular.

~~~~~~~~

At six foot five inches in heels, Genesis commanded the stage. She was a true queen in every respect. Despite the nearly two foot tall butterfly precariously perched on her head she effortlessly glided to the microphone. She surveyed the audience. Her drag shows drew an eclectic crowd, mostly regulars, to the club. She spied James Cooper, alone at a corner table. As a mistress of transformation, James' attempts at disguise always made her smile. *Looks like I'll be pocketing a nice chunk of extra cash tonight. Just need to find someone with thick skin and a need for money more than morals,* she thought.

Genesis elegantly waved her long silver nails, introduced the next act, and backed off the stage. She entered Miss Muff's dressing room. "I have a special job for you this evening right after the show."

Miss Muff turned away from the mirror. Her gruff voice inquired, "Should I bother taking off my makeup?"

"That won't be necessary. Pick out a dress you don't care about and have some Advil handy," Genesis instructed.

# FORTY-FOUR

"Winston!" Lolly called out in an exasperated tone.

Winston appeared at his mother's side. "I am right here."

"Oh, thank goodness. I just need to be sure you have this information." Lolly shook the paper in her hand and laid it down on the kitchen counter. "I've been like a whirling dervish getting things ready for our trip to France. You would not believe the amount of work I've had to do. It's just so—"

Winston cut her off before she went on a tirade about how hard it was to get the staff to perform in a timely manner. "Yes, Mother, you work very hard. I will miss you very much."

His comments pulled her attention back to why she had called Winston to her in the first place. "Oh, I hate leaving you here all alone."

"This happens every year, Mother. I will be fine."

His mother waved a dismissive hand and continued with her speech, "Yes, well here is what you need to know. Chef has stocked the freezer with ready-made meals. The staff is coming with us but I've hired a cleaning crew to come on Mondays. Here's their number. Also, the grounds people are here on Tuesdays and Thursdays. Their phone number is here too. The cleaners and the groundskeepers are the only people with the entry code to the front gate. The cleaners have a key to the house. They are very trustworthy. Still, I've locked up the silver and my jewelry and I would appreciate if you could be present in the house when they are here on Mondays. If your schedule allows, of course, darling."

160

Winston simply smiled at his mother and asked, "What time are you and Father leaving?"

"The transport is picking us all up in an hour. Now give me kiss. I must go supervise Sally moving my bags. We will phone you when we arrive."

Winston bent toward his mother's cheek. "Travel safe."

# FORTY-FIVE

Jack McCarthy, Officer Sanders, and Captain Todd all stood in front of a full wall-sized whiteboard speckled with photos, notes and a timeline.

Captain Todd gestured at a photo of Ken. "Talk to me. I want to know who Ken Tate was."

Jack began his narrative. "Ken Tate. Thirty years old. He grew up in Newton, MA, and Florence, Italy; which is where his mother and father live now. He's an only child. Ken went to private boarding school here in New England, Deerfield Academy, and graduated from Tufts University with a degree in Business Administration. His dad was a wine importer and mom stayed home. Ken borrowed money from a small Rhode Island bank, that's long since been acquired by bigger banks, to start up his venture capital business Spinnaker Ventures. He was also the primary investor in starting up a computer application business, Diamond Enterprises, with his college buddy Jared Diamond. No girlfriend, hard to find any friends that knew him socially. Most people knew him through business, and he has no family around here."

Officer Sanders jumped in. "In fact, a representative of the family contacted us just after the news of his death went public. They want to know when they can send someone in to clean out his place and take the body back to Italy for funeral and burial."

Captain Todd glanced between the two men then asked, "Have we completed a search of Mr. Tate's home?"

Officer Sanders answered, "We finished up with Ken Tate's condo but didn't turn up anything."

"Okay, tell the family they can have access to the condominium." Captain Todd looked back to the whiteboard. "Autopsy is complete. We can go ahead and release the body." Both officers nodded as Captain Todd continued. "McCarthy, your friend, Maddie Marcelle, says she saw Ken using a cell phone at the party. But no phone was found on the victim."

Jack McCarthy stepped to the whiteboard. He pointed to a cluster of pages hanging on the board with a magnet. The word 'phone' with a question mark was written in red marker above the pages. "Right. There was no cell phone recovered from his body, his office, his car, or his condominium. We pulled all his phone records. We got one number which reoccurs on his office line and cell phone pretty frequently." Jack tapped the pages for emphasis on his next piece of information. "Most importantly he got a call from that same phone number on the night he died. That number was the last phone call to come through. The call lasted one minute and thirty-four seconds and the timing for that call was just before the established time of death."

"Okay. So who's number is it?'' Captain Todd asked.

Jack McCarthy's frustration was exposed as he twisted his lips. "That's the problem. It goes to a disconnected line with a 'number no longer in service' message. We tried tracking it but it's a dead end. The number goes back to a pre-paid burner phone with no registered user."

Captain Todd crossed his arms over his chest, "Anything else? Give me something."

Officer Sanders offered, "Okay, according to phone records, a final text message was received on Ken Tate's cell phone from none other than Jared Diamond, also close to the time of death, demanding that he and Ken Tate needed to talk."

Jack let out a sigh. "Well, we know that Jared and Ken had a connection, we know they had a fight, a text message doesn't really help us out. But we do know he was keeping secrets if he had a burner phone."

Captain Todd pointed back to the whiteboard, "Let's dig deeper into Spinnaker Ventures. It might give us a lead. Maybe he had a business enemy at the gala?"

# FORTY-SIX

Jack shook out a dish towel as Maddie handed him a final pan to dry. Kelly leaned on the counter opposite them in her kitchen. The dinner conversation between the trio had mainly focused on the murder investigation.

"Coffee's ready," Kelly announced. "Let's go have it in the living room."

Kelly and Jack took up seats on their couch with Maddie in a soft armchair opposite them.

"I keep coming back to a few things," Maddie said. "Bob was asking me about Ken during the party then I saw him follow Ken outside."

"Yeah, but he explained he went outside to smoke and he was interested in Ken as a business contact," Jack interjected. "We don't have information to contradict his story at this point."

"Okay. I also come back to something Ken said. He implied he was dating or seeing someone in secret and the person is a public figure." Maddie heard a voice she had not heard in a long time, not Kelly's voice, not Joe's, but her own. "Listen, Jack, I can use my connections with Bob and Jared to find out if there is more information." Jack opened his mouth to speak but Maddie quickly continued. "I promise not to do anything stupid or dangerous. If I hear information or see anything questionable I will pass it on to you."

Kelly could tell from Jack's expression he was considering her point and piped up. "We can't stop her from dating Jack."

"True. I'm not investigating. I'm just dating," Maddie added to reinforce her point. "Besides I want to help out. It makes me feel stronger."

Kelly tipped her head. "What are you talking about, stronger?"

Maddie set her coffee cup down on the table in front of her. She leaned forward as she rested her forearms on her knees. She felt compelled to dig her fingernails together but resisted the urge. "Until now, I haven't felt comfortable sharing this with you both. My relationship with Joe really undermined my confidence in myself. I came to depend on him too much. I allowed him to control me. It's been a process but I am learning to trust my own decisions again. Honestly, spending time with you both has helped a great deal. Even dating has shown me I don't need to be afraid to make connections with people. I'm adjusting to everything I have. I'm giving myself permission to learn from my mistakes and not shut down and hide from the world."

Kelly dropped to her knees next to Maddie's chair and engulfed her in an embrace. "You are not alone Maddie. You're stronger than you know and when you doubt that, Jack and I will be here to remind you." Maddie watched as Jack nodded his head in agreement.

"Are you okay?" Kelly asked.

"I am actually feeling so much better," Maddie said.

Kelly returned to her spot on the couch next to Jack. "Good. Let's make a plan." Kelly stated.

Both women fixed their gaze on Jack.

"Okay let's be clear. You two are not cops. But I have to admit it might be helpful, Maddie, if you were to host a little couples dinner for me, Kelly and Jared at your house. So you can be dating, and I can be investigating."

"Oh no! I can't think of anything more awkward," Maddie exclaimed.

Jack surrendered his hands to the air. "I won't be overtly interviewing the guy. As a matter of fact, I promise to play the part of good friend, not bad cop."

Kelly gave them both an eager smile.

Maddie couldn't hide her energy either. "Let's do it!" she exclaimed.

# FORTY-SEVEN

Maddie pulled away from Jared's embrace as she heard her mudroom door close. Jared laced his fingers through hers and clasped her hand tighter as Jack and Kelly appeared in the kitchen.

Kelly waved a bottle of wine toward Jared and Maddie. "Jared, we have you to thank for introducing us to our new favorite wine, Pinot Gris."

The tension of Jared's grip let up only slightly as he spoke. "Glad I could be of service."

"I'm just going to address the elephant in the room." All eyes went to Jack as he spoke. "This is obviously an unusual situation. Jared the most you and I have ever talked has been at the police station. We all know you and Ken were close friends and this is a terrible loss for you. I am not here tonight as a detective. I'm here as Kelly's fiancé, Maddie's friend, and a guy that wants to get along with you. I can separate my job from my personal life." Jack's hand jutted forward and hung in the air waiting for a response from Jared.

Jared separated from Maddie and took up the handshake. In a relieved tone he stated, "I would like to give it a try. Honestly, I want answers just as much as you do, Jack."

~~~~~~~~~

Two bottles of wine down, the dinner talk had covered many subjects, but not the murder. Still it was clear to Jack, Maddie, and Kelly that Ken's death had a deep impact on Jared.

The conversation halted as Jack looked down at his ringing phone. "It's the station, I gotta get this." Jack stood up and walked toward the kitchen. The cottage's open floor plan allowed the others to keep eyes and ears on Jack.

"Something Diamond's auditors found? ... A lead through Spinnaker Ventures to an account –hold on let me write it down." Jack looked back to the dining table and signaled Maddie for paper and pen. She quickly delivered him what he needed. "Yeah go ahead. Royal Cayman Bank. Okay, I'll do some checking on my end." Jack clicked off the call and looked at Jared. "We need to talk."

# FORTY-EIGHT

"**P**lease come in Mr. Lackey. Mr. D is ready for you." Mikey stood at the open door like a bull waiting to charge a matador; forcing Bob to turn sideways as he passed into the office on Federal Hill.

"Nice to see you again, Mikey," Bob commented as he squeezed by. Bob was a pretty good poker player but this meeting would require every bit of bluffing skill he had. *Game face. This is the break I need to get in good with Cosimo. I got this.*

Cosimo DeCastelleri was back behind his desk. He pointed to the opposite chair, indicating Bob should sit down. "What's this about Ken Tate?"

*Down to business,* Bob thought. "Okay. So you know I got connections down in Newport. Well, I got invited to one of those fancy society parties at one of the mansions down there. I happened to meet up with Ken Tate. Who's working on one of your projects." Bob paused to see if he had pushed a button with Cosimo. *Wow,* he thought, *Cosimo really should've been a poker player.*

Cosimo continued to stare at Bob. "Go on," was all he said.

"Me and Ken, ya know we really hit it off. We got to talking about stuff and figured out we both have a connection with you." *So far, so good. Mostly the truth. Here we go.* "He told me was gonna set up a meeting to bring me in on the project with you. He thought cause of the people I know down in Newport I could be a big help." *Poker face, sell it.*

"So what did Ken tell you about our project?"

170

Cosimo's face gave nothing away but the inflection in his voice as he said the word 'project' let Bob know this was something worth pursuing.

"Not too much, cause he went and got himself killed. But I know his friend, Jared Diamond, and since Ken's out of the picture I figured I would be the perfect person to take over the job."

"What do you know about Diamond?"

"Well, I know that Diamond doesn't know Tate was working for you. Ken and I talked about keeping his association with you just between us."

Cosimo listened, his face expressionless except for his eyes which gleamed like the point of a dagger.

Bob felt Cosimo's eyes boring through his skull to read his mind. *God, I hope he believes this bullshit.* Bob tried to clear his head, terrified that Cosimo could actually read his thoughts.

Cosimo slowly turned his chair and gazed out the window. Custom made. The glass was bullet proof but the style was correct for the architectural history of the building. He abruptly snapped his head around to face Bob. His sudden movement caused Bob to sit back a bit further in his chair.

"Sure Lackey, you can take over. Let me set some things up. I want you to call the new number I gave ya in one week. Then I'll give you instructions." Cosimo stretched his arm across the desk and held his hand out to Bob. *"Prego.* Welcome."

Bob stood. A grin spread across his face as he shook Mr. D's hand. "Great, this is great. I can take care of business. You'll see."

~~~~~~~~

Bob was practically skipping down Atwells Avenue. He still had no idea what Ken was doing for Cosimo but he was about to pay his friend Moe a visit to find out. *I can't believe Mr. D is bringing me in on a real freakin' job! Jared Diamond's the key to this project. The best way to get to Diamond is through my little princess, Miss Maddie.*

# FORTY-NINE

A bell tingled on a door announcing Bob's entrance into Moe's Electronics store in Cranston. He gave Moe a friendly nod and they headed behind a heavy black curtain strung up behind a display counter.

Bob loved visiting the back room of Moe's shop. It always reminded him of the last few pages of a comic book; filled with ads for gadgets that promised to enhance your spy powers and strength, so you too could be like your cartoon heroes.

"Hey Moe, are these x-ray glasses?" Bob held up a pair of thick-rimmed eyeglasses.

"No. They're binocular glasses."

Bob settled the spectacles on his nose.

Moe chuckled. "Now push the logo on the side of the frame. See, it lets you zoom in and out."

"This is so cool!" Bob exclaimed. He inspected a pen. "What's this one do?"

"That's a good one." Moe plucked the pen from Bob so he could demonstrate. "Not only does it write, it's got a camera in it so you can record."

Moe inspected a tall metal shelf with labeled plastic drawers. A near-by workbench was cluttered with household items, sculptures, and stuffed animals. All were in various states of disarray waiting to receive hidden recording cameras. "I assume you want something small?" Moe called out.

"Yeah smaller the better and I'm on a budget." Bob continued to fiddle around with a teddy bear.

"Ok, this one." Moe held up what looked like an iPod with earbuds in one hand and something small, shiny and round in the other.

Bob came in for a closer look. "What is that, a quarter?"

"Exactly. But this coin's superpower is it can transmit to this iPod. It's got decent range, so you won't need to be right on top of whatever you're trying to hear. But it doesn't record, it just lets you listen."

"Perfect," said Bob with a grin.

~~~~~~~~~

"He's a friggin' liar, Mikey!" Cosimo hissed.

"So why not just take care of him now, Mr. D?

"Because, Mikey, I want to know how much he really knows about our project and if he's said anything to Diamond. I know he's involved with Ken's death. So I'm gonna give him a little rope, so he can hang himself. Have him tailed. I wanna know every move he makes."

# FIFTY

Bob stood up as Maddie approached his table at an outdoor café just off Bellevue Avenue in Newport. Maddie set her cup and saucer down next to his and allowed him to give her a warm hug. Bob always liked to start a conversation with a lady with an obligatory compliment, in Maddie's case he actually meant it.

"You look beautiful, as always, Miss Maddie." *Now for the set-up.* "Thanks for meeting me here, Maddie. I know I haven't had time to take you out on another proper date but my schedule's been a bit crazy lately. I also know I need to make time for what's important and you're important to me, Maddie."

Unlike Bob, Maddie was not at all sure about how important Bob was to her. Her inner voice was speaking up. She had become more confident listening to it. It was telling her Bob was a lot like Joe. His lines seemed smooth and practiced and he was all too confident about the effect he could have over her. Bob's glance down at his phone to check the time cemented her suspicions she was being played. "Bob, I have to be honest with you. I'm not really sure about your definition of making time for me because I literally have not heard from you, not a phone call, not a text, from the time I saw you at the gala until you asked me here today. It's been weeks!"

Bob studied her face as she spoke. *She is really hot. But time is wasting here. Great segue Miss Maddie. Let's get down to business.* "Yeah, sorry for the incommunicado situation. Like I said, I've been real busy with work. So speaking of that fancy party murder, how's the investigation going?"

175

Her invisible antennae twitched. She was grateful to know her intuition was still there. *Fishing expedition. Ok, I'll bite.* "I'm not sure, Bob. I'm not a detective."

"But your friend Jack is. He must've said something about it. I heard the cops were looking into your other friend too, Jared Diamond. He and Ken were good friends, right? Business associates?"

"You seem pretty interested. Maybe there's something you want to tell me?" Maddie retorted.

"I don't know, Maddie." Bob offered up a shoulder shrug. "Of course I'm interested. I was at a party where a guy I had just met turned up dead a few hours later."

"Funny, I don't remember seeing you again that night after Ken Tate was found," Maddie pressed.

"Come on. What is this an interrogation? I gave my statement to the cops. You really want me to go over it again?"

Maddie noticed Bob's usually suave and confident demeanor had turned edgy. She decided to zone in on this opportunity to expose what she felt was a hole in his story the night of the murder. Joe might have screwed up her ability to trust own decision making, but right now it was her instinct she trusted and it was telling her Bob was hiding something. "Well, I wouldn't mind you telling me why I saw you following Ken outside, not long before he was found murdered."

"Look, I told the cops and I'll tell you, I went outside a bunch of times to have a smoke. If Ken was outside too, it was a coincidence.

I never saw the guy out there." Bob tapped his finger on the table to the slow count in his head. He needed to stay in control. He opted to deflect and press on to the next order of business. "So you know the art business seems to be pretty hot right now. I was thinking, maybe we could do a little business together?"

Maddie sat back in disbelief at how he could flip the subject of their conversation. What he said next was even more incredulous.

"If you front me around ten grand, I would have it on hand, so if I see a piece that looks like something you would be interested in I could get it right away."

Maddie nearly choked on her coffee as she was caught off guard by his absurd proposal. The look on her face made Bob realize he was experiencing a very rare moment. He had actually misread how far he could push his good graces with a woman. He could feel his window of opportunity closing. He had to act fast. He shot his arm forward toward his coffee cup. It hit his intended target. Maddie's purse spilled to the ground with a thunk.

"Maddie I'm so sorry. I'm such a klutz today." Bob was under the table in a flash. "Here, let me just put your stuff back in your purse."

"No. I've got it." Maddie leaned over to pick up the bag.

Bob had only needed an instant to slip the listening device into her purse. Maddie re-adjusted some of the items in her bag while Bob continued to apologize. "Let me get you another drink, make up for my being so clumsy."

Maddie couldn't hide her annoyance as she quipped, "Really, now you want to buy me a drink? Two minutes ago, you wanted me to give you a pile of money. I'm sorry Bob, I have no problem helping out my friends when they are in need but I don't get the sense you're actually in need or that you're truly interested in being my friend."

"You're right, Maddie I want to be more than your friend." *God, it's not like she's strapped for cash. Why is she acting like such a bitch?* Bob could feel his frustration and anger rising. He tried to cover it and stay cool but his charm was slipping away. "I'm sorry I asked for financial help. I just thought we could work something out like a loan or maybe a good business deal for some art. But if it's gonna be a problem for our relationship, then just forget about it."

Maddie was incensed that Bob was trying to make her a bad guy. "You know what, Bob? I am going to try to forget about it. I have to go. I have an appointment." Maddie was up from the table and away before Bob could even think of a response.

# FIFTY-ONE

Not since before the gala had the faceless man who haunted her dreams appeared. But tonight she was again visited by a sense of foreboding, and this time she was awake and aware that her instincts were now intact. *Maybe all those nightmares weren't about the past,* she thought. *Maybe they're a premonition. Maybe they're a warning.*

She checked her rearview mirror again to see if the headlights which had followed her through the last two turns continued to keep pace. *All clear. Ok, better lay off the James Bond movies for a while.* She made the final turn onto what served as the small village of Jamestown's main road and looked for a side street to park.

Bob knew when to hang back to avoid being spotted. He eased the car he had borrowed from Moe up a street that ran parallel to the one he had seen Maddie pull onto and park. He hopped out and deftly bolted through the backyards separating him from Maddie. He dropped to a crouch as he nestled up alongside her car. He peered up and down the road. There, just a few paces away he spied her. She was approaching a streetlight at the crossroad which would bring her to the main street. Bob quickly picked his way along the yard side of the hedges which lined the road. He was close to the ground, tucked behind a shrub at the corner of the road as he watched her head onto the main street and walk into a small restaurant a few doors down. Bob retreated back to his car and moved it into position, closer to the restaurant, so he could listen.

Thanks to the listening device he had planted, Bob had heard Maddie's side of the conversation as she made plans to meet up with Jared. Unfortunately, she never said where they were going. Bob adjusted his earbuds. Fortunately for him, Maddie and Jared were in a small, quiet restaurant. The ambient noise wasn't too loud. Bob increased the volume on his device and was met with crunching static. "Damn it!" he cursed. At that moment the static stopped and Bob was rewarded with the sound of Jared's voice.

"I have no idea, Maddie, why Ken would steal money from the company. He gave me the money to start the company!"

The crackle was back but only for a few seconds. Bob again heard Jared's voice.

"Like I told Jack when we were at your house, I've never even heard of the Royal Cayman Bank."

The static had started again but it didn't matter that the device had stopped working. Bob had heard enough. He yanked the earbud wire out and pounded his fist on the steering wheel. "The islands!" Bob exclaimed aloud. "Cosimo had been talking to someone on the phone about the islands when I was in his office. I'm a betting man and I bet that scumbag Ken was embezzling money for Mr. D." Bob rhythmically tapped his fingers on the wheel as he continued to think aloud. "I know just how to collect on Mr. Tate's misfortunes. It seems my dead buddy Ken and I are about to take our partnership to the next level."

# FIFTY-TWO

B ob thanked Moe for facilitating a meeting with Jimmy the Creator. As his name implied, Jimmy was a master creator of official documents, notarized papers, and false identifications. Jimmy had advised Bob on the paperwork he would need for his project and Bob was confident Jimmy would supply him with everything he needed. However, it would cost a pretty penny.

Bob drove away from Moe's Electronics lost in thought about how he would come up with the money needed to pay off Jimmy the Creator. *Didn't go too well last time I tried but maybe some time away from my awesomeness has made Miss Maddie wax sentimental. Bet I could squeeze a little cash out of her for this job. I'd like to squeeze something else on her too. That girl's got some willpower. I can't believe she's been able to resist me this long.*

Bob's machinations led to a lapse in his usually cautious driving. He hadn't bothered to check his rearview or side mirrors, so he never saw the car following him since he pulled out of Moe's Electronics shop.

# FIFTY-THREE

Maddie smiled and waved as she headed past the front desk of the animal shelter. "I'll see you next Thursday, Kate."

"Thanks again Maddie for all you've done over the past few weeks."

"No problem, Kate."

In an instant, Kate was up, around the corner of the desk and touching the sleeve of Maddie's shirt. "Maddie, it's not just the money you donated. Although, God knows it was needed and you are an angel. But I want to thank you for the time you have put in volunteering here."

"No need to keep thanking me. It really is my pleasure, Kate."

As Maddie drove away she thought out loud about what she had just said. "It really is my pleasure. I never had a pet. Who knew I would like working with those animals so much? And everyone I've met there is genuinely nice."

Her ritual of self-reflection was interrupted by a loud ringtone reverberating through the inside of her car. She let the call ring once more as she debated answering it. *I know what I need to do,* she thought as she tapped a button on her steering wheel and took the call from Bob. Maddie could not keep the irritation from her voice. "Hi, Bob."

"Hey, Miss Maddie. How the hell are ya?" came Bob's cheery response.

"What do you want, Bob?" Maddie asked.

"Okay, well let's get right down to business then. So, last time we were together I floated the idea of us collaborating on some art purchases. I thought maybe you might be ready to make an investment? Like maybe something around three grand?"

Maddie quickly pulled her car to the side of the road so she could set Bob straight. She purposely spoke at a slower pace and enunciated each word. "Bob, listen to me. I need you to actually listen to my words. I am never going to do business with you. I am never going to give you money. I am no longer interested in having a relationship, a friendship, or even a passing acquaintance with you. You should delete my phone number as I never want you to call me again. Do you understand?" Maddie's stomach formed a tight, nauseous knot as she braced herself for the blowback.

Bob's tone was low and smooth. "I'm not gonna lie, Maddie. I'm sorry things aren't gonna work out between us. But maybe it's all for the best. I have some business opportunities overseas, so I won't be around for a while anyway. Thanks for the good times. Bye."

The line went dead. Maddie stared at her car's screen where the Bluetooth call had been connected. She let out a long breath of relief. *That was so much easier than I ever thought it would be,* she thought.

~~~~~~~~

*Wow, that girl's got a screw loose. Oh, well, saves me from swimming in the deep end of the crazy pool. Looks like I better give Betty a call,* Bob thought as he scrolled through the contacts on his phone to call Mrs. Vanderbeck.

# FIFTY-FOUR

Sounds of a throaty singer twisted with the slow twang of acoustic guitars. The rhythm danced across the harbor from Fort Adams and glided around Maddie and Jared. Maddie clinked her wine glass to Jared's. They sat shielded by weathered, wooden shingles from the bright sun of the day.

"Your porch has got to be one of the best spots to listen to the Newport Folk Festival!" Maddie exclaimed.

"Well, we could've been down there on a boat," Jared stated.

"No, this is better. I like being up here, above the fray, taking it all in."

"I'm glad you're happy Maddie."

Maddie noticed Jared's tone had changed. He suddenly sounded melancholy.

"Jared, what's wrong?"

"Nothing is wrong..." Jared had started to object but the look on Maddie's face told him she wasn't buying it. "You're right, I'm a little sad today."

Maddie watched him and waited.

His stare was trained out across the harbor. After a few moments, Jared issued a monotone list. He let space hang between each statement. "I used to watch the folk festival with Ken. Some days are better than others. I fluctuate between angry and sad. I have questions that may not be answered." Jared snapped his head to face Maddie. His voice rose as he continued. "Not to mention I'm still a person of interest with the police. Ken was keeping secrets from me. Me, his closest, possibly only friend in the world!"

Maddie spoke softly, "I know how hard it is to lose your best friend. I know I've alluded to my difficulty dealing with my breakup from Joe and losing Mr. Whitmore. I've struggled to make decisions, to find things I enjoy doing by myself, not to fear making mistakes and to trust myself. Just telling you this is a big leap for me. I know what it's like to hold secrets. Maybe you know more about Ken's secrets than you think. Maybe if you talk about him, you might remember some detail that will help bring his killer to justice."

Jared shook his head left and right. "I believe you mean well Maddie. But it worries me that you keep involving yourself in this case."

Maddie's body drew away from Jared toward the back of her chair. "Why are you worried?"

Jared suddenly stood up and firmly stated, "I don't want to talk about this anymore. I'm going to get us another bottle of wine. Let's just enjoy the view and the music, okay?"

She looked after Jared as he stepped off the porch and disappeared into his house. It was hard to watch Jared's mood swings. Yet, she understood all too well what he was going through.

# FIFTY-FIVE

Maddie doubled over and clenched her stomach. Winston was next to her laughing just as deeply as she. She flipped her head up. Her face was flush, tracks of sweat ringed her face. "I don't think I will be playing Wimbledon anytime soon."

"Oh, come on now Madison, you're doing just fine. Just try to keep the racquet in your hand next time."

Maddie caught the white towel Winston tossed her in mid-air.

"See? Your hand-eye coordination is improving too," Winston joked.

He took up her hand as they exited his tennis court and strolled along a path toward his main house.

Maddie gave his hand a squeeze. "Thank you. I feel like I haven't laughed like that in ages."

"I told you learning to play tennis would be fun."

Maddie smiled. Without thought, her next words slipped out like a breath of air. "It's just so easy being with you."

"As opposed to being with Jared," Winston prodded.

Maddie stopped in her tracks. Sadness flashed across her face as she answered him. "Sometimes. I know you don't want to hear this but the guy is really torn up about losing his best friend."

"Well, Madison, you might not want to hear this but that's not a reason to stay with him."

Maddie's tone was defensive as she explained, "Winston, we've talked about this. I'm not ready to be in an exclusive relationship, yet.

I enjoy spending time with you and with Jared. I'm sorry if I implied differently."

"Madison, I don't want to fight with you. I know how you feel about jealousy. I assure you, I'm not jealous. However, I do care about you. I want you to be happy. It was my fault for bringing up Jared. I hope you will accept my apology. Today is just about us."

Maddie's gaze locked with Winston's. She didn't want to fight either. "Apology accepted," she said.

"Good," Winston stated. He pointed to their right toward stone steps which wound down to the ocean cove and a small boathouse. "Would you like to go out on the boat or head up to the pool?"

"Pool, please. Maybe some margaritas?"

"Don't forget, Madison, I'm all alone in the house. Everyone has gone to France."

"Seriously Winston, you need staff to make margaritas for you? Let me take this opportunity to teach you something. Margaritas are my specialty!"

~~~~~~~~~

Maddie pressed her lips on Winston then turned to face the stunning color display of sunset. "This is my favorite time of day. Magic Hour. A time for possibilities," she whispered. Mr. Whitmore had given her the term 'Magic Hour'. Every day she and Mr. Whitmore would sit together at twilight. The only rule for their conversation during that time was it had to be positive. The good energy of things to come or fond memories of the past. Some days the light show was more spectacular than others. But every sunset with Mr. Whitmore was a magical time.

"Would it be possible for me to take advantage of Magic Hour and ask you to stay here with me?" Winston asked.

Maddie gently traced a finger along Winston's strong jawline. "I'm sorry. I'm not ready for that yet. Besides, I'm meeting Kelly early tomorrow morning."

Winston gave her a final kiss before she headed out of his house.

"Text me first thing in the morning," Maddie called out as she opened her car door.

"I always do," he answered back then closed the hefty front door.

Curved thickets of beach roses and thick shrubs guided her way down the long driveway. She braked at the substantial iron gate separating her from Ocean Drive. She knew the gate would open automatically, as no code was needed to leave the property. Her eyes shifted to her rearview mirror. But for its dramatic sloped, slate roof and many stone chimneys, Seafair was now barely visible.

She basked in the last rays of the sunset over the water as she made the short drive back to her own home off Bellevue Avenue. "Thank you, Mr. Whitmore. I am happy," she said aloud.

# FIFTY-SIX

M addie put her hand on the knob and twisted. "It's locked."

Kelly turned up her palms as she asked, "Did you expect it to be open?"

"I guess we could call the condo association and give them a story about why we need to get into a dead man's condo." Maddie suggested.

Kelly held up two pointed instruments that looked a lot like knitting needles. "We could, but this will be easier." Kelly hovered over the lock on the door to Ken's condominium. "Something Jack taught me a while ago after I got locked out of our house."

Maddie watched Kelly's tinkering. "How you doing there, Sherlock?"

"Quiet. It's not an exact science you know." There was an audible click. Kelly beamed. "Here we go."

The girls quietly stepped inside and scanned around.

"Not much in here," Kelly commented. "Ken's family cleaned the place out as soon as Jack cleared it from the investigators."

"Do you know anything about Ken's family?" Maddie asked.

"Not much. Jack said his parents are in Italy. The police have been dealing with a family representative to claim his body and take care of his estate."

"Given that we just broke in, I take it Jack doesn't know we're here?"

Kelly crinkled her nose. "If we find something, then we will cross that bridge; for now, it's just between you and me."

"I'm on board with that, Kelly." Maddie instructed Kelly to start taking the drawers out of the cabinets. "My mom taught me this trick." They moved through the kitchen pulling drawers completely out of the cabinetry. "Every time we moved. See, people always check to see if a drawer is empty." Maddie used her phone's flashlight to peer around the wooden cabinetry cave. "But often times, stuff in a crowded drawer will fall behind it."

Kelly mimicked Maddie's search skills. "What are we looking for?"

"I don't know right now. But anything we find could be something that helps."

"Do you want me to go check the bathroom and look in the toilet tank?" Kelly joked.

Maddie gave Kelly a serious glance. "Yes, I do. Remember *The Godfather*? Go tear that bathroom apart."

~~~~~~~~

"Maddie! Maddie! Get in here!" Kelly shouted.

Maddie rushed into the bathroom.

190

Kelly pulled a photo out of the void left by a vanity drawer she had removed. "It must have slipped out from the back of a drawer," Kelly said from her seated position on the tile floor.

Maddie bent over her shoulder so they could scrutinize the picture. "That's definitely Ken," Maddie commented.

"Yeah but the face is ripped off the guy he's standing with," Kelly noted.

"Did it tear off behind the drawer?" Maddie asked.

Kelly flicked her phone's flashlight around the small square space of open cabinetry.

"Do you see the rest of it?" Maddie urged.

Kelly twisted the light around inside the vanity opening, "No, nothing else down here."

The girls resumed their examination of the photo showing Ken standing next to a faceless upper body.

"Mountains in the background. Close angle. Looks like a selfie?" commented Kelly.

Maddie pointed. "Definitely. Look at the man standing next to Ken. The way the guy's head is torn off. It's very precise."

Ken's unknown companion had an arm draped around Ken's shoulder.

Maddie tapped the photo. "Hey, look at the faceless guy's hand. He's wearing a ring. Can we magnify this? Or make it clearer?" she asked.

Kelly nodded. "Yes, when we turn it over to Jack."

"Check the back," Maddie directed. "Maybe there's a name or a date."

Kelly flipped the picture over. For a moment the girls were speechless as they read each other's stunned faces.

Maddie slowly shook her head from side to side. "It can't be."

"Oh, it very well could be." Kelly countered. "We know they were best friends. Maybe they were a lot more to each other?"

Maddie looked at the back of the photo again. The letters K and J were written with a heart drawn between the letters.

Maddie stood up and rubbed her forehead. "I'm dating Jared. I'm developing feelings for Jared." Maddie shifted restlessly as she grappled with the implications of the photo. "There's more to this. We can't just assume."

Kelly looked up at Maddie. "Do you think they were in a relationship? Maybe Ken had unreciprocated feelings for Jared."

"I don't know Kelly. I don't know what the hell all this means." Her controlled tone was tinged with anger. "But I will tell you, I damn well will get to the bottom of this."

# FIFTY-SEVEN

Officer Sanders circled the station's fishbowl. He could tell by the gesturing going on inside the room Detective McCarthy wasn't very pleased with the two ladies sitting at the table.

"I don't need you two out playing Nancy Drew and Veronica Mars!" Jack McCarthy gave each woman a pointed glare.

Kelly and Maddie waited until Jack had turned to look out of the fishbowl's window before they gave each other a troubled glance.

Jack caught sight of Officer Sanders and waved him into the room. "Officer Sanders, this is my fiancé, Kelly Hurley and our very close friend, Maddie Marcelle."

Officer Sanders extended his hand to each woman. "I've seen you both around the station for your statements with the Tate case. It's nice to meet you both."

"Kelly and Maddie are responsible for recovering the photo of Ken Tate from his condo," Jack stated.

Unlike Jack, Officer Sanders looked impressed. "That was quite the find, ladies. I thought our team had gone through that place pretty thoroughly. The lab is analyzing the picture now. Maybe you two should be consultants on the case?"

Wrong thing to say. Jack looked at all three of them and gave an emphatic, "No! Look this is a murder investigation. This is not a game. This is a dangerous situation."

"Jack, we're sorry to upset you. We do know this is a serious matter," Kelly offered.

Jack let out a deep sigh. "I'm not mad, I'm worried about keeping you both safe."

The room fell silent as Jack paced back and forth before he continued. "It's bad enough you're seeing Jared and Bob, two men who might be involved in this murder." Jack pointed an accusing finger at Maddie.

"Well, one out of two. Bob might be involved but I have nothing to do with him anymore," Maddie stated.

"What happened?" Jack asked with concern.

"A problem I never thought I'd have. Someone who was more interested in my money than in me. I cut him out a couple weeks ago," Maddie answered.

At that moment another officer knocked on the fishbowl door. Jack McCarthy waved her in.

Jack introduced Officer Terry. She set an open laptop computer down on the sole table in the room. "So, after we eliminated Ms. Hurley and Ms. Marcelle's prints we were left with only Ken Tate's prints on the photo." She tapped a few keys on the computer and brought up an enhanced copy of the backside of the photo Kelly and Maddie had found. "Given the prints, it seems Mr. Tate was the one who wrote on the photo." Officer Terry clicked another key. An enlarged version of the faceless man and Ken Tate appeared. She zoomed to the hand of the faceless man. "Good eyes spotting the ring," she commented. Kelly and Maddie tried not to smile. "It's the only distinctive feature we have of our faceless man; other than that, he's about the same height and build as Ken Tate. Also, the picture seems to have been taken recently."

Officer Sanders spoke up, "If I may?" All eyes turned to him as he continued. "My understanding is that all three of you now have a degree of personal relationship with Jared Diamond." The group nodded in accord and Officer Sanders went on, "At this point, I think using your connections with Diamond might be helpful. Especially as it relates to this photo you found. It might be the break we need."

The focus went back to Jack as he acquiesced, "Okay, but we all agree that any information, even something as small as a discussion about taking selfies with Ken Tate, gets reported."

# FIFTY-EIGHT

Maddie beamed. "Thanks for meeting me, Jared."

Jared's lips quickly brushed hers. "This is fun. I don't mind being a tourist and roaming Cliff Walk."

"Yeah, this is a great place to walk. It's especially fun when you get out toward Rough Point and you have to crawl over the rocks. I would imagine it's a lot like hiking in the mountains?"

Maddie focused on Jared's eyes to see if he would take the bait. She wasn't entirely comfortable questioning Jared. She was less comfortable with the idea Jared and Ken's friendship may have been much more or that he might actually be a killer.

"I've actually never made it down that far on Cliff Walk."

Maddie hoped he would add more information. Nothing. She again tried to float a lure, this time she decided to be more direct. "Have you ever done any mountain hiking?"

"Yes. Back in college. Ken and I used to hike up in New Hampshire."

*The photo of Ken was more recent than that*, she thought. "So, were you and Ken always just friends in college?"

Jared shook his head gave a laugh of disbelief as he answered, "What else would we have been?"

"Oh, maybe you had a tutoring relationship or athletic rivalry, or something else?"

Jared's expression conveyed his confusion. "I don't know where you're going with this, Maddie, we were friends. Best friends."

*I don't know where I was going with that either*, Maddie thought. New tactic. "Speaking of Ken, did he have anyone special in his life?"

Jared came to a halt as he addressed her. "Police asked me that too. No, he did not have a girlfriend. To my knowledge, he wasn't dating anyone. What is going on with you?"

Maddie thought fast. She didn't need a lie. "Something just popped into my head. It was something Ken said to me the night he...well, the night of the gala."

"I'm listening," Jared said.

"He told me he had someone special in his life. Someone he was seeing privately but the person was someone the public would know."

Jared tipped his head back and laughed.

"Why are you laughing?" Maddie practically screeched.

"Because he was teasing you, Maddie. He was probably talking about me. You didn't know him the way I did. He was always looking to get a rise out of people, stir up trouble, create mystery, and he loved double entendre. That's something he would say to draw you in to try to get to know him better. That's all. Don't read into it."

Maddie couldn't help but blurt out what was going through her head. "But what if he was talking about you, Jared, because he had feelings for you?"

Jared's face darkened, his lips formed a serious line. "That's not okay to ask, Maddie. He was my best friend. Don't try to turn it into something else. I told you I was worried about your involvement with the investigation into Ken's death. This is one of the reasons. You trying to force me into a conversation that I am not going to have."

The look of Jared's anger had melted into hurt. She knew she had pushed him too far. "You are so right, Jared. I should never have asked that. You lost your friend and instead of support, I'm giving you more grief. I really care about you and I am so sorry."

Jared spun away from her and ran his hands through his hair. When he turned back to face her she desperately scanned his eyes. "This is hard, Maddie. But I really care about you too. I think we can be good together. Let's just stop talking about Ken and let the police do their job."

Maddie agreed and allowed him a long, deep kiss.

# FIFTY-NINE

B ob lifted his straw fedora and mopped the sweat from his forehead. He had been here for two days scouting out his mark. He watched the bucktoothed girl leave the Royal Cayman Bank. He was feeling pretty confident about his approach. He adjusted his hat and followed her into a coffee shop.

"EEE!" the bucktoothed girl shrieked as ice and tea dripped from her arms.

"Oh, I am so sorry!" Bob exclaimed. "Here, let me help." In an instant, Bob was caressing the girl's arm with a napkin. "Please, let me buy you another one," Bob said connecting with her eyes. "In fact, maybe we could sit down and I could join you?"

~~~~~~~~~

*Not an attractive girl, but definitely the right girl,* Bob thought as they continued their conversation.

"So, you're just in town for one night, Mr. Peters?" the girl drawled out.

"Right, I just got here and I need to close out an account at the Royal Cayman Bank tomorrow for my business partner. Hopefully, I brought all the right identification and paperwork. Please, call me Robert."

"Oh, my gosh! You're not going to believe this Robert, but I work customer service at that bank."

"Well, that is a coincidence. You know, I'm on my own for dinner tonight. Perhaps you could recommend a good spot?"

The bucktoothed girl's body floated toward Bob. Her mouth was slightly agape as she stared at him. "The Painted Palm is really nice," she said.

Bob met her stare and cast deep into her eyes. "I'm very much looking forward to doing business with you tomorrow." *Time to reel her in,* he thought. He laid his hand over hers and whispered into her ear, "but maybe tonight we could do something more personal?"

The bucktoothed girl's cheeks grew hot and colorful. She gave him an enthusiastic and breathy, "Yes."

Bob pushed a napkin across the table to her. "Write down your number. I'll call you when you get out of work."

The girl's hand shook with excitement as she wrote her number. "I'll see you tonight. I've got to get back to the bank," she said.

~~~~~~~~

Bob entered the bank at 9 a.m. Armed with fake photo identifications, a notarized proxy giving Ken's business partner, Robert Peters, access to his account, and a few other official documents which Jimmy the Creator had insisted he needed.

His bucktoothed customer service girl looked pretty groggy. Understandable after the night they had.

Twenty minutes later, Ken's account was closed and Bob was a wealthy man.

~~~~~~~~

Bob shook the last of the money bundles from his satchel onto the bed of his rented Cayman bungalow.

"I'm rich!" Bob called out. "I win, Cosimo! This time I win." *Now, where will I go next?* he thought. He spied some travel magazines on the bedside table and flipped the pages. He paused at the advertisement and said aloud, "Monaco. Nice. The casinos are supposed to be off the hook there."

"'You're the only one who is gonna be off the hook when I feed you to the sharks out here!'"

Bob dropped the magazine and spun around. He watched in terror as Cosimo DeCastelleri and Mikey stepped inside the bungalow bedroom door. Cosimo held a gun with a suppressor aimed at Bob's heart.

Bob began to shake and sweat as he looked at the gun then down at the piles of cash spread across the bed.

Bob's hands were in the air, his eyes and fingers both opened wide. He tried to sputter an explanation, "Look, Mr. D, I was gonna bring you back the money. I was just thinking I could make more of it at the casino. You know, give you a bigger payoff."

"Shut up, you stupid piece of shit. This isn't about the money. Five years I've had to put up with you because of a promise I made to my uncle. But you know what? I'm an uncle too. Unlike you, you lazy bastard, my nephew was smart. It was his idea to create a business that could launder the family's money. Filter it into legitimate establishments. That fucking computer company was gonna be a gold mine. We could just take some right off the top and keep it here in paradise," Cosimo said.

Bob's mind reeled as he tried to put together the pieces and spoke,"Computer company—"

Cosimo cut him off. "I don't fuckin' care about that company now! I got plenty other businesses to pick up the slack. This is about family, honor, and revenge for my nephew. Ken Tate was my sister's kid."

The information hit Bob hard but not as hard as the bullet that tore into his chest killing him instantly.

~~~~~~~~~

Cosimo tucked the arms of his sunglasses behind his ears and looked at Mikey as they exited the Royal Cayman Bank. "That went well. Money talks, Mikey, but that bank manager sure won't."

Mikey nodded in agreement.

"It's nice here," Cosimo commented looking around at the swaying palms. "I like those trees, we should get some of them for my office."

# SIXTY

"The New York Yacht Club brunch does not disappoint," Winston commented as he and Maddie walked down the club's dock.

"I'm so full I may have to swim home," Maddie joked.

As they approached their boat a voice called out, "Hey, Big Jay."

Winston turned toward the voice. "I'll be damned, Michael, how are you?"

Winston and Michael locked in a sturdy hand grip. "Michael, this my friend Madison Marcelle."

"You can call me Maddie," she invited as she shook Michael's hand.

Michael smiled and clapped Winston on the back. "It's been a long time, my friend," he said then turned to Maddie. "We were at Deerfield Academy together and this guy was a record-setting quarterback for our team. He was a football beast."

"And you were just a beast, Michael."

"Oh behave! What are you up to?" Michael inquired.

"Madison and I are going to take the boat around the point back to the dock at the house."

Michael nodded. "One of the Newport greats. I haven't been there in years."

"Well, we're going to have a quiet romantic late dinner since we have the house to ourselves tonight. But why don't we meet here tomorrow for drinks? Just us guys and we can get caught up. You don't mind, Madison, right?"

"Of course not," Maddie answered.

"Great plan. Where's your boat? I'll cast you off," Michael said.

"The Morris, right here." Winston pointed to the boat.

Michael untied the line from the cleat and helped cast off the boat. Maddie and Winston gave a hearty wave as they pushed off the dock.

# SIXTY-ONE

Jared stared at his computer screen. It was another Sunday alone at his office. He clicked his computer keys with one hand as the other absently searched for his coffee cup.

"Damn it!" He called out as coffee seeped through his shirt. He angrily stripped it off, yanked open his closet and tore through hangers to find another shirt. His hand gripped a tuxedo jacket. He flung it aside much too hard as the jacket flopped off its hanger and landed on the floor with a thud. *What the hell was that?* he thought.

He picked up the tuxedo jacket and began crunching material between his hands. He felt a hard lump and reached deep into an inside pocket. He pulled out a cell phone. His head slowly turned to look at his desk where his cell phone was sitting. *What the hell is this?* he wondered.

He opened the phone and scrolled through numbers. What jumped out at him was the fact all the numbers were the same. *This is crazy. One number, no name attached, just unknown caller.*

Jared touched the camera icon on the screen. "Shit!" He leaped to his desk and dialed the phone, urgently repeating, "Pick up, pick up, pick up." Voicemail. He dialed another number this time he got an answer. "Jack, we need to talk now!"

# SIXTY-TWO

Winston turned a key; with a low rumble, the engine of his sailboat purred like a panther. "Nice thing about this boat engine, it is quiet enough to have a conversation not like those boorish cigarette powerboats," he commented to Maddie as they headed away from the dock of the New York Yacht Club.

~~~~~~~~

Winston was at the helm carefully turning and adjusting the wheel as he dodged dangerous rocks to navigate into the protected cove where his boathouse was perched.

~~~~~~~~

He leaped from the boat onto his dock and secured the boat.

Maddie tossed him another line from the boat's deck as she asked, "Winston, why did Michael call you big Jay?"

Winston held out his arms and assisted Maddie from the boat onto the dock. "Growing up my parents opted to call me by my middle name, Winston, but as luck would have it there was another Winston in my class at the Academy. So to save confusion, I went by my first name at school. James."

# SIXTY-THREE

Jared pounded his hands on the table in the police station's fishbowl room. "Come on Jack, we don't have time for this," Jared erupted.

Jack's mind was churning. He knew this was a significant break in the case. He was mindful to speak in a calm manner. "The prints came back on the phone. Just yours and Ken's. There's only one number ever called or received on the phone. The phone itself is a burner phone. More importantly, there is a text from the one number the night of the murder demanding a meeting at the teahouse. It stands to reason whomever the one phone number belongs to is probably our killer. It could also go to another burner phone and be a dead end. It's going to take a little time to trace it. Now, tell me why you have a phone with Ken Tate's prints on it."

Jared's hands were behind his head, he was quickly pacing a line along the table. Exasperated, he answered, "It's not my phone." He reached into his back pocket and threw a cell phone onto the table. "That, right there is my phone. Go ahead and check it, but we don't have time—"

Jack needed to keep Jared focused. He knew all too well what needed to be done and how potentially perilous the situation could be. "Jared, we are working on it. Please get back to how you found the phone."

Jared took in and let out a deep breath. "I found it at the gala. I had just argued with Ken. We got a little physical. He had a grip on me and I had grabbed his jacket half off. He walked away. I saw a phone on the floor. I picked it up. I checked around in my pockets and my phone was missing. I figured it was mine so I stuck it in some pocket of my tux. There was a lot going on that night, you know. I didn't think about it again. But this is not what's important. It's the picture!"

"I know Jared, we're trying to call her again."

Jared pleaded, "Can't you trace her phone to locate her?"

"We've already got that started," Jack answered.

The fishbowl door opened. Officer Sanders announced, "Sir, we got your fiancé on the phone."

# SIXTY-FOUR

Maddie pushed into the stone and shingled boathouse. She was hit by a wall of dank, humid air. "I'm going to open some windows in here," she called out.

Winston's shadow filled the doorway. "I will get us some wine."

The pair moved out of the boathouse and took up seats on the terrace overlooking the dock and jagged cove below. As they sipped their wine they casually relived the events of the day.

"It's so secluded and peaceful here," Maddie observed. "I could get used to this."

Winston grinned. "I hope you do."

Maddie leaned over to Winston and gave him a kiss.

# SIXTY-FIVE

Jack lifted the handset of the phone hanging on the wall in the fishbowl. "Kelly, I'm at the station with Jared. I'm putting you on speaker phone."

Jared swiftly stepped to the phone and called out, "Where is Maddie?"

"Why?" Kelly asked. "Is something wrong?"

"Just answer the question!" shouted Jared.

"Hey, calm down," Jack admonished. "Kelly, we found a phone. Based on prints it seems to belong to Ken Tate." Jack held up a hand to prevent Jared from interjecting. "It's a long story. Bottom line is there's a photo on the phone of Ken with—"

Jared couldn't hold back any longer. He urgently blurted out, "Please Kelly, where is Maddie?"

"She's with Winston. They were going out on his boat this afternoon," she answered.

The door opened again to the fishbowl. Officer Sanders reported, "Jack we got a GPS location on that cell phone."

# SIXTY-SIX

"**B**ottle's empty. Would you like some more wine?" Winston asked.

"Sure." Maddie stood up. "I'll get it. You're not used to manual labor," she giggled.

Winston flashed her a grin.

She selected a bottle from the mini refrigerator situated under a long, room length counter which served as a bar and a boat utility catch-all.

"Do you have a wine opener?" Maddie called.

"Try the top drawer under the counter," answered Winston.

She opened the drawer, fished out the wine opener. Her eye caught sight of something in the drawer. "What's this?" she said and held up a ring.

# SIXTY-SEVEN

Jared faced Officer Sanders and asked, "Where is she?"

Officer Sanders frowned and looked at Jack. He was not sure if he should be giving the information directly to Jared.

"It's okay," said Jack. "You can tell us."

Officer Sanders spoke, "GPS shows Madison Marcelle's cell on Gooseneck Point off Ocean Drive."

# SIXTY-EIGHT

Maddie walked out onto the terrace. "What's this?" she asked, holding out a ring.

Winston plucked the ring from her hand. "Oh, my family ring. I forgot I left it here." He looked it over then slipped it onto his finger. "Makes sense, though, I don't like to sail with it on. I'm always afraid it might get caught when I'm hauling in a line. It usually turns up between here and the boat. Thanks."

Maddie's face paled. She stared at the ring on his finger. "I know that ring," she said.

"You probably do. I might have had it on last time I saw you," Winston stated.

"No, that's not it. I've seen it in a photo," Maddie said with determination.

"Okay. I don't understand why you look so confused Madison?"

She stepped back from Winston's chair. Maddie's mind raced as she put the clues together. *Because you're J. K heart J you're the missing face from the photo.* She blurted out, "You knew Ken!"

213

# SIXTY-NINE

Jared nodded his head and gave the table a quick hard slap. "I gotta go."

"Hold on!" Jack stepped in front of Jared before he could reach the door. "Where are you going?"

Jared gave Jack an incredulous look then briskly answered, "To get Maddie at Winston's house. She is possibly in a lot of danger. We now know that Winston knew Ken. He's been lying about it. Come on, Jack! Winston is in a photo with his arm around Ken on a burner phone with Ken's fingerprints all over it!"

Jack tried to reason with him. "Jared, you're not a cop. This is a dangerous situation for you too. We've already sent a couple officers over to pick up Winston for questioning. It looks bad but a photo on a phone doesn't make him a killer."

"Then why didn't Winston tell anyone he knew Ken?" Jared retorted.

"I don't know. That's one of the questions we'll ask him," Jack responded.

"I gotta go." Jared side-stepped Jack and pulled open the door of the fishbowl.

Jack reached out and grabbed Jared's arm. "Wait."

Jared met Jack's eyes. "Am I under arrest?"

Jack released Jared's arm and stated, "No."

Jared bolted from the room.

# SEVENTY

Winston looked up from his chair toward Maddie. He shielded his eyes from the glare of the sinking sun. "Honey, what are you talking about?" he asked with surprise.

Maddie's voice became louder, "I don't understand, Winston. Why did you act like you had no idea who Ken was at the Marble House party? When you had obviously taken a photo with the guy!"

Maddie stepped back inside the door of the boathouse. Winston was up and walking to her.

"Madison, you're not making any sense. What's this photo? And if I'm in it then why haven't the police asked me about it yet?"

"Because your face is torn off!" Maddie yelled.

Winston moved toward Maddie. She retreated backward further into the room. The small of her back jammed into the counter. She could retreat no further. Winston stood over her, reached down, and picked up the wine opener. Maddie's breathing was audible as she nervously watched Winston drill the sharp, spiral metal spike into the yielding cork and pour himself a glass of wine. He took a long drag from the glass then looked down at Maddie.

His voice was low as he slowly spoke, "So that I have this straight, you saw a photo of me with Ken but my face was torn off. So why on Earth would you think it's me?"

Maddie thought her heart might pound out of her chest. Winston's hand came up toward the side of her head. She arched her body back further over the counter. Winston snapped a switch behind her and the boathouse was illuminated.

"It will be dark soon, Madison, and we clearly have a lot to talk about."

Outside the boathouse, the sky was deepening through shades of purple. Maddie was scared but Winston seemed so calm. *Please help me, Mr. Whitmore, to figure this out,* she thought. Then another thought came to mind. Maybe she was wrong, maybe it wasn't Winston in the picture. *Oh no! What if it was Winton's father?* "I... I'm so sorry, Winston," Maddie sputtered. "I saw the ring and it's the same as the ring in the photo and I thought it was you."

"You thought it was me Madison because I have a dark colored ring? A lot of men have dark colored rings, like high school rings, athletic rings. So where is this incriminating photo of yours?"

Maddie wanted to trust his explanation. She wanted to tell him the truth but the instincts she had suppressed for so long were screaming in her head. She lied. "I don't know, it's somewhere at my house."

"Where did you get this photo? Does anyone else know about it?"

Maddie felt compelled to lie again. "No. No one knows about it, yet. I found it when I was digging through Ken's empty condo."

Winston looked at her quizzically. "Why would you do that, Madison?"

"I don't know. I thought I could help with the investigation."

Winston shook his head. "So, you presume that because you have a friend who is a detective that you too are a sleuth? Come on Madison. You're being ridiculous. Let's just drop this." Winston picked up his wine glass and finished his drink.

Maddie's nerves were on high alert. Her thumbnail was excavating under her other fingers. Still, she needed to know more. She remembered the ring in the photo had a distinctive crest. She was sure it was the same as the Cooper family ring. "I studied the ring in the photo Winston. It's your family ring and Ken is in the photo."

The color in Winston's face suddenly darkened from a soft pink to crimson as he bellowed out, "For Christ sake, Madison, I didn't know Ken! And I certainly never had a picture taken with my arm around him! Now just fucking drop it!"

Madison's voice was just above a whisper. "I never said you had your arm around him."

# SEVENTY-ONE

A t the same moment, Officers had arrived at Winston's address. Officer Terry rang the buzzer on the gate and looked at her partner. No answer. Her partner reached out and pushed the buzzer several times in a row. Nothing. They walked along the dense privet hedge separating the estate from the road.

"House is up there, but it's pretty hard to see in," Officer Terry noted. They tried to part the hedge to get a better look.

"Fencing inside these bushes goes all along here. Stops up at the rocks and water," her partner added.

The officers walked back to the main gate. Officer Terry made a decision. "Yeah, it's all dark up there. He's not here. Let's go. Maybe they have a number for this guy at the station. We can try to get a location off his phone."

# SEVENTY-TWO

Maddie tried to move to her left but Winston sidestepped directly in front of her; the counter still pressed into her back.

"You're not going to drop this, are you? Damn it Madison! I wanted it to be you. I wanted to build the life I am supposed to have with you! But you just won't stop digging and I can't have that. You want the truth?"

Maddie was terrified, but she needed to know what was going on. She swallowed hard, nodding her head up and down. She managed to get out the words. "I just want to know what happened."

~~~~~~~~~

Jared's grip on the steering wheel had turned his knuckles white. He directed his car around the winding curves of Ocean Drive. He had a pretty good idea where they were, he just hoped he was in time.

~~~~~~~~~

"I'll tell you about what happened, Madison. I'll also tell you about what's going to happen." Winston lurched forward, grabbed Maddie's arm and spun her around. From behind, he rammed her chest into the counter and held her in place with his body. He snatched a piece of rope from the counter and tied her wrists together, behind her back.

Maddie cried out, "Winston, stop! What are you doing? I just want to talk!"

Winston turned her around to face him. His eyes were wide and intense. He bent closer to her face and hissed, "No, I'm going to talk. You're going to listen. Someone has to listen!" He shoved Maddie toward a small wooden chair and forced her down onto it.

~~~~~~~

*Locked gate, thorny tight hedges, fortified with an iron fence,* Jared noted as he surveyed the entrance to Seafair. He jumped down onto the beach at the head of a cove adjacent to the estate. *This is the only way in,* he thought. He would have to make his way over the jagged rocks along the shore to gain access to the property.

The clear night sky and bright moon allowed him some visibility. Jared kept his body hunched low and began the treacherous climb along slippery, seaweed clad spiky rocks.

~~~~~~~

Winston composed himself as he glided a hand over his mouth. He nodded his head and looked down at Maddie. "Yes, I knew Ken. I met him years ago at Deerfield Academy. He was a year behind me. We always kept our association private. He and I had an arrangement, on and off, over the years. He understood my dating women was, well, necessary. You see, in order to inherit my family's billions, I must comply with the terms of our family trust. I must be married, to a woman, and produce biological children. Otherwise, the money passes along to my cousins. Ken was my lover. And although times have changed, the terms of my inheritance have not. Ken knew all about you.

221

I told him. I thought you, Madison, I thought you were that special woman. The woman I was to marry."

Maddie held her breath and tried not to recoil as he ran a single finger down the side of her cheek. He spread his finger and thumb across the breadth of her neck. "Now, obviously, I'm going to need to start again!"

Maddie's eyes wildly followed him as he moved about the boathouse. "What are you going to do, Winston?"

"See, Madison, you remind me of Ken. Always pushing me, questioning me. 'Why can't we be together?' 'I have enough money for the two of us.' " Winston skidded to a stop in front of her chair. "As if he knew what real money is. As if he had any idea of my lifestyle or the power." Winston placed his hands on his hips, hinged at the waist and looked into Maddie's terrified eyes. "He actually tried to blackmail me into staying with him!" Winston rose back up to his full height. "Ken thought he had been following me in my black Range Rover." Winston smirked. "Turned out, my dad had been taking my car to visit whores working as massage therapists. When Ken figured it out he tried to use my father's activities to trap me in a relationship. He threatened to leak information to the press about my father if I didn't come out and be with him." Winston dropped to squat and clenched Maddie's knees. He pleaded his reasoning. "I tried to break it off, to control myself but he was going to ruin everything. I had to stop him."

"So, you killed him the night of the party," Maddie quietly said.

Winston seemed intent on making her understand. "I could manage Ken dancing with you. But when he approached my father, with you in tow, it was the final straw."

222

Maddie's disgust boiled up into her voice. "You murdered him. Then went right on pretending. You have no soul, Winston Cooper. You're a monster!"

"Perhaps," he said quietly. "Now let me think." Winston popped back up to his feet again. He resumed his pacing around the room.

Maddie eyed the door. It was dark outside. She knew he was fast and strong. She wouldn't be able to get far if she tried to run. Maybe she could reason with him. "Think about what, Winston? You can't kill me. It's not like the night you killed Ken. People know we were out on the boat together. There are witnesses."

Winston snatched up a rag and stuffed it into Maddie's mouth. "There. It's so much better when you can't talk."

The oily cloth assaulted her senses. She tried to work her tongue to push the greasy rag from her throat and mouth.

"You're right Madison, lots of people know we're together. Lots of people also know you are a novice on a boat. Accidents happen all the time on boats." A malevolent smirk turned up the corner of his mouth. Winston's beamed with the brilliance of his plan. "Yes, boating accidents happen all the time. Tonight's accident will just be more tragic than most. You see we are going to go on a romantic starlit cruise." Winston's face was instantly in front of hers. He continued speaking with mock drama. "When suddenly we hit a rock here in the cove. You'd been drinking, the toxicology report will back that up. You were thrown to the side of the boat on impact, where you hit your head." Winston arched his back and was up again. His words excitedly flowed. "I was dealing with the hole that opened up in the hull from the crash, as it was causing us to take on water. Unfortunately, when I looked up I realized you must have fallen overboard. I search for you. I call loudly, for the benefit of anyone on shore to hear of course. I call a mayday on the boat's radio for help—'The boat is sinking and a passenger is missing!' I dive into the water with a flashlight, trying desperately to find you. I will still be frantically searching when the Coast Guard arrives. Sadly, they find you dead." The edge of Winston's finger again grazed Maddie's cheek. This time she winced. Winston's story continued in a self-satisfied tone. "What they will never know is that you were already dead when I brought you on board. Then all I have to do is ram my boat onto a rock, throw you over, and wait it out. Salt water tends to muddy up even the best coroner's timeline. And the rope marks on your wrist are easily explained by your dangerous handling of the lines. Bad sailor, wrapping them around your palms and wrist for leverage, rookie mistake on a boat."

Maddie's horror reached a fever pitch. She knew his plan would work.

~~~~~~~~

Jared clambered onto the grass from the rocks below. He could see light radiating from the boathouse. As he swiftly closed in he could hear Winston's voice. He ducked low and silently approached an open window.

~~~~~~~~

Winston loomed over Maddie with a bottle of wine. He ripped the rag from her mouth. Before she could take a deep breath she was choking on the wine Winston was pouring down her throat. "Can't have fibers in your mouth, might mess with my story. Let's go!" Winston yanked Maddie up from the chair.

Maddie was spitting, coughing and gasping. She struggled to get out her words. "I thought you were going to kill me?"

"Yes, but not until we get down to the boat. Ties the forensic evidence together and saves me having to haul your dead weight around." Winston pushed Maddie in front of him toward the door.

Jared needed to act fast. His hands darted along the ground. He grabbed a loose rock, wound his arm back and prayed his pitching skills would not fail him.

"AHHH!" Winston doubled over in pain grabbing his shattered elbow.

Maddie did not know what had just happened but she knew she needed to move. She lurched for the door but felt herself toppling forward. Winston had reached out and caught her leg. With no hands to break her fall her head slammed onto the hard wood floor. Winston was on her, his body weight cemented her to the floor. His one hand gripped the front of her throat and started to close like a vice. Suddenly air exploded out of her lungs and she could breathe. She rolled over and saw Jared's fist crash into Winston's face. Winston lay motionless.

# Aftermath:

Jack, Kelly, Jared, and Maddie sat around the table in the station's fishbowl.

Jack smiled at Maddie and Jared. "You two are very credible witnesses. The judge is holding Winston without bail. I think our case is pretty tight now," Jack said. "I also wanted to let you know we checked up on the account at the Royal Cayman Bank that Ken had opened. We spoke to the bank manager, he said he personally closed out Ken's account after Ken died. Apparently, Ken had opened the account to help out his family. Two of his cousins came in and closed the account out. The bank manager said they were headed back to Tuscany."

Jared let out a sigh and rubbed his forehead.

Jack continued. "It's your call Jared do you want us pursue this?"

"No. I know Ken's family, they're a proud people. It's just sad to me Ken felt like he had to steal the money to help them out. If he had just come to me I would've given it to him, but I understand when pride gets in the way. Besides, his family's been through enough and I don't need the money." He rubbed Maddie's hand between his palms, "I've got everything I need right here."

Maddie smiled and looked at each person at the table. "I have friends, I have money, I have you, but I might need a therapist."

Made in the USA
Middletown, DE
02 August 2021